FAE'S SONG
FATED MATES OF THE FAE ROYALS
SUMMER COURT BOOK I
HELEN WALTON

Walton House Publishing

www.helenwaltonauthor.com

CONTENTS

FOREWARD

Choosing character names isn't always easy, and there are times you pick them to mean something for the character and the story. I've included the pronunciation and meaning of the names, and if you're like me, and like to know and still pronounce the names the way you read them, then welcome to my club.

Niamh pronounced neeve meaning radiance.

Fintan pronounced fin-tan meaning white fire.

Eamon pronounced aim-on meaning keeper of riches.

Maeve pronounced may-veh meaning intoxicating.

Diarmuid pronounced deer-mid meaning without enemy.

Orlaith pronounced or-lah meaning golden princess.

Rian pronounced ree-an meaning little king.

Briana pronounced bree-a-nah meaning noble.

Aislinn pronounced ash-lin meaning a vision or dream.

Saoirse pronounced seer-sha meaning freedom.

Lorcan pronounced lor-can meaning silent or fierce.

Ciara pronounced key-rah meaning dark.

Roisin pronounced roe-sheen meaning little rose.

For the fire will burn with the white brilliance of love

PART ONE

A FATED LOVE

CHAPTER ONE
NIAMH
IRELAND 1400

THE AIR IN THE barley field shimmered with a claret haze like tiny droplets of crystalized blood. Father and Mother stopped in their tracks and focused on the veil separating Earth and the Summer Court. The rippling claret curtain sent a quiver through my body. It was a rare sight to see in our remote location and meant only one thing. A Fae royal attendant was about to step through the veil.

The wind rustled the golden stalks, expectation building in the air and along every inch of my skin. A tall man appeared through the magic and bowed his head respectfully.

"Mr. and Mrs. O'Keefe," he greeted. "I am Grieg, King Diarmuid's royal aide."

"Greetings." Father tipped his head, then scratched his ginger beard. "How may we be of service to the King?"

Grieg withdrew a scroll from the breast pocket of his red coat. "The King requests a performance for the Prince's two hundredth birthday ball."

Father unraveled the parchment and scanned the words, his eyebrows rising to within an inch of his ginger hair. "His request is for our daughter, Niamh?"

"Aye."

Grieg flicked his gaze to me, standing on the edge of the field a few paces behind my parents.

"Not me?" Mother placed a hand to her throat as though they had taken her beautiful singing voice from her. She was renowned for her singing, from our small village, and the ones closest to us, to the big city. Invitations often arrived asking her to perform. The King should have asked my mother, not me.

"The King has heard your daughter has a special talent for singing and he'd like nothing less for his son on his birthday."

"Father, I can't," I stammered.

"It's a royal summons, Niamh. We can't ignore it," Father said.

I shook my head. "I can."

"No," Grieg said, his lips forming a tight line. "Attendance is mandatory."

A moment of silence descended as that piece of information settled in my ears and brain.

"Very well," Father said. "She'll be there."

Grieg bobbed his head and strode the short distance to me. "A pleasure to meet you, Niamh. I'll be your escort to the party."

I dipped my head as they expected, but my lips firmed into a tight line.

Grieg's passive expression didn't change. "I'll return in an Earth week."

I shoved my knuckles into my mouth.

Grieg waved his hand in a glowing claret arc and parted the veil back to the Summer Court, leaving as suddenly as he'd arrived. The veil snapped shut a second before the wind dropped. The barley ceased rustling. My heart hammered inside my chest.

"Shite," Mother said.

"Aye, a fine mess," Father said. "We have no choice but to send Niamh—to deny the King is unheard of."

"But..." I said.

"Your father's right, you have to go."

Mother strode over to me.

"Perhaps it won't happen this time?"

I choked out a laugh. "You know it will."

Mother sighed and cupped my cheek.

"I'm sorry, Niamh. If I could figure out a way to turn it off then, I would."

"What if my voice affects more men? What if someone gets hurt again?" I struggled to breathe through the tightness in my chest. "I can't keep doing this."

"I don't know, sweet child, but you are more than your voice. One day you'll find a true mate and it won't matter how many men you lured with your song."

"The King is an honorable man. He wouldn't allow any harm to come to you in his kingdom." Father cleared his throat and thrust his hand over the barley stalks. "What do you think of this crop? Will it make the best lager?"

A small smile tugged at my lips. "Aye, Father."

He eyed my dress. "I suppose you'll need a new gown for the ball?"

I shrugged my shoulders. The last thing I wanted to do was to sing in front of the royals. As much as I loved singing, the unwanted attention my voice produced in men sent a shiver of dread through my body.

"I'll start on one," Mother said. "Purple? You look lovely in purple."

"If you like." I spun and walked in the opposite direction to our home.

"Niamh, where are you going?" Mother called.

"A walk." I pointed at the forest.

"Niamh, let's talk about this."

"Let her be," Father said. "There's plenty of time."

"A week is not long enough." Mother sighed. "Then there's the dress to make."

I continued walking, their voices growing distant with each step. The barley field disappeared as I entered the forest. The tall trees cast a gloomy shadow over my heated flesh. They should soothe as they usually did, but the coolness wrapped around my aching chest and dragged me down into the depths of despair. I couldn't do this. I couldn't sing in front of so many men. If my voice didn't lure men and trick them into believing I was their mate, then I'd jump for joy at this opportunity.

The last time I'd sung for a small crowd, one man was more determined than the others I was his and wouldn't believe I wasn't. My repeated 'no' had landed on his unhearing ears. My eyes misted as the image of my injured father, battered and bleeding while trying to protect me, seared into my mind and sat like a heavy stone on my shoulders.

Around me, the trees creaked. The skin on the back of my neck prickled. I scanned the treetops. Nothing moved. Ahead, the forest path separated in a fork. No movement there either. To go left, or right? It didn't matter, so long as I didn't head home to the fuss of Mother making me a dress for a ball I didn't want to attend.

"Which path will you choose?" a female voice drifted from the treetops.

I stopped at the fork and searched the branches. The leaves rustled like a wind stirred them, but there was no wind today except for when the King's royal aide stepped through the veil. I half expected another Fae to appear. When nobody appeared, I took a step toward the path on the left. My foot slipped on the bright green moss underneath the trees. I swung my arms and stayed upright.

A cackle breezed through the treetops.

"Who's there?"

My voice weaved through the trunks of the forest. I'd learned from the day I spoke my words wielded power in song. A Fae power so unlike other Fae powers. One passed down to all females born in my family, but not all had the other power I dreaded.

"Your destiny lies the other way," the woman said.

I stepped to the right path. My foot once again slipped on the moss, but this time I didn't keep my balance and landed on my butt with a squeal and a thud.

The woman laughed at my expense.

"Whoever you are, stop this," I shouted.

"I can't stop what I'm not doing," she said. "We all have a path laid out for us."

"I'm destined to be this way? Or go this way?"

Who was she? Elf? Woodland Sprite? Witch? Pixie? Too many possibilities. I scrambled to my feet.

"Aye," she said, her voice growing faint as though she were moving away from me.

"Wait. What's my destiny?" I wiped my hands on my dress.

The rustling of the leaves ended, and her voice fell silent. I searched the surrounding forest from top to bottom. Whoever was out there had left. *Strange woman*. I walked the path I'd come from. Back to home. Was my destiny at home?

I hummed as I walked. More often than not, I'd sing safe in the knowledge we lived far from others and no man would succumb to the lure in my voice. With a strange woman in the forest today, I needed to be careful.

The door to our thatched white cottage stood open. Mother's soft singing drifted out. I stepped inside to a flurry of indigo, lilac, and purple fabric.

"About time," Mother huffed. "Talk to me."

"I don't want to talk. There's nothing you or anyone can do to help me." I slumped into a chair. "I should never have sung at the fall festival."

"If it hadn't been the fall festival, you would have sung somewhere else at some point in time. I understand all too well the force inside us urging us to sing." She flicked at a swath of indigo fabric. "Besides, we didn't know for certain you had the luring power until that night."

What a disaster of a night. My voice had ensnared many men in the village, and they'd all demanded I was their mate. A fight had broken out. Father had broken it up and been injured in the process. The requests for my performance had trickled in since then. We'd kept them local, made sure the men knew ahead of time they might act strange to my singing. It hadn't stopped them from falling for the lure and declaring I was their mate, but it had stopped further fights from breaking out. But this performance...

They wouldn't be aware of the luring power in my singing. And Mother only told those she trusted to keep it a secret.

"What if I ensnare every single man in the Summer Court and they fight over me?"

"The King has his guards. You'll be safe in the Summer Court." Mother pointed at the fabric. "Which color?"

"Any."

Mother held the swatches against my body. "Lilac."

I fingered the delicate fabric. "Will it be enough for the Summer Court?"

"I'll add to it."

"Mother." I clasped her arm. "I don't want to go."

She placed her hand over mine. "Our family has avoided the Summer Court because of our unusual inherited power, and the rumors about our heritage, but the Spring Baile heals Fae. What if you're meant to go? What if the spring's water can heal you?"

"I'm not hurt." I stepped out of her touch.

"No, but you are hurting."

My spine stiffened. "How would I get to the spring?"

"The spring is located inside the palace. It is the life force of all Fae and the Fae Royals' sacred duty to protect it. With the ball and the number of guests I'm assuming will be there, you might be able to slip away unnoticed for a little while."

"That seems wrong, Mother."

"It is our spring, too. It shouldn't matter we live on Earth. We are Fae too."

"Aye." I nodded. "I'll see if I can find it."

Mother held up the fabric. "We'd best get started on the gown."

I held my arms out and let her take my measurements, contemplating her words. What if the spring's water stopped the lure in my voice? It was worth going to the ball just for the chance of curing my condition.

"You know the Royals are special. Their power commands all the elements, unlike every other Fae who only command one element," Mother said.

"I've heard they're beautiful, too."

"Oh, aye." Her eyes glazed over. "I saw King Diarmuid last time he visited Earth. My goodness, beauty and masculinity all rolled together."

"Mother," I gasped.

"One can appreciate beauty from afar."

"I'm sure Father would be happy about that."

Mother scribbled numbers on a scrap of paper. "The Queen enamored your father too."

I rubbed my forehead.

"I hear the Prince is more handsome than his father."

"You've never seen him?"

"No." She flicked the fabric in the air and settled it over the large wooden table. "You'll have the chance to see for yourself at the ball and when you return, you can tell me if the rumor is true."

I scoffed. "I have no intention of looking at any man."

CHAPTER TWO
FINTAN
THE SUMMER COURT

T HE BOISTEROUS GIGGLES OF the Fae women grated on my ears. I left the banquet hall before another woman fluttered her eyelashes and smiled in a way that let me know they'd be more than willing to trade their bodies for a crown. Their voices, high pitched with excitement, sent dread through my veins. Soon, I'd have to choose one of them to be my mate. Forever.

I glided through the elaborate marble halls of the Fae royal palace, heading away from my party. Quiet was impossible with the bedlam of the ball. I required a moment of solitude. I entered the seclusion of the atrium in the palace's heart. The gentle trickle of the spring falling over smooth rocks to gather in the pool below gave me the peace I longed for. The soft scent of the array of white, fluffy blooms drifted down from the ceiling. All around, nature thrived in sprigs of glossy green plants and an abundance of flowers. The Spring Baile, our Fae spring of life, welcomed me, its protector. I heaved a deep sigh. Instead of the usual scent of the powerful water, earth, plants, and fresh air, a sweet aroma teased my nostrils.

Amongst the abundance of blooms, a Fae woman kneeled at the bottom of the spring. She gazed into the magnificence of the water, unaware I'd entered the atrium. The light of the glittering moon bounced off the running cobalt liquid of the pool and highlighted the contours of her delicate features. She was exquisite. She leaned forward and scooped a hand into the water. Her silvery-yellow hair fell forward over her bare shoulders in soft waves. The woman could almost be a royal with her pale skin and silky silvery hair, except she wasn't. I was the single heir to the Fae throne. She lifted her cupped hand and sipped the water with her pursed lips.

The sight of her lips sent heat through my veins.

Why was she here in our most sacred place, drinking from the spring?

"Who are you?" I walked closer to the woman who enchanted me without the need for words, fluttering eyelashes, or pointless giggles. I drew her sweet scent in again, which left me with nothing but warmth running through my body. My powers surged and sensed no malicious intent or harm to the spring from the Fae woman. As a royal, I'd sworn to protect our sacred spring. That duty would come first.

Her dainty shoulders jerked. She lifted her head, long dark lashes fluttering over eyes the color of crushed blue moonstone. They held me hostage and burned into my mind. Her pink lips pouted in a perfect ring. Desire punched me hard in the groin to claim them—claim her.

"What is your name?" I whispered the words through the tightening in my body.

She gazed up with wonder flashing in the depths of her eyes, as all Fae did upon seeing a royal. Emotions flittered across her face, but she didn't speak. She blinked, and her expression settled into one of wariness while I battled a torrent of passions and the urge to kneel at her feet.

She licked her plump lips and scrambled to her feet, deciding for me. The enchantress lowered her eyes and bobbed a curtsy. I clenched my jaw.

"Don't," I rumbled, and tilted her chin up with my fingers. "I entered the atrium to avoid everyone treating me like a prince."

My power rippled hard and intense through my skin on her flesh. *Mine.* The conviction of it raced through every nerve in my body. She flicked her wide blue eyes to mine. Ah, she experienced the connection too.

She dropped her gaze to the floor.

"Lady, I require no subservience from you."

She stumbled back out of my reach. Her bare feet padded on the cobblestones.

"Of all the..." I caught both of her arms in a gentle grip. Uncontrollable power coursed into my palms and warmed against the silky material of her dress, seeking her flesh underneath. "You don't need to be afraid of me. I won't hurt you."

Her bottom lip trembled. *Why wouldn't she talk to me?* An unfamiliar stab of emotion poked me in the chest. I dropped my hold on her again.

"Has someone hurt you?" I glanced at the doorway of the atrium. If any of the guests in the grand ballroom had hurt this sensitive creature, I'd rip them limb from limb.

She shook her head, soft curls caressing her bare shoulders. Shoulders I wished to stroke with my hands. Her gown was resplendent, a lilac bodice with intricate gold stitching hugging her curves and breasts, shoving them up into twin mounds of creamy skin. My mouth watered.

I sighed. Lust wasn't a new sensation to me, but this was more than the attraction of her body. *Is this intense power coursing through me every time I touch her the force of my mate?* I stalked away from her and paced the atrium back and forth once, twice, before I regained control of my powers and settled in front of her again.

Her body trembled, but she met my gaze. *Did she still fear me?* The notion sent panic to clench in my stomach. I didn't want my potential mate to be frightened by me.

"Come, sit with me." I sat on a large boulder and waved at the space next to me. "My name is Fintan."

She flicked her gaze to the door before settling on a boulder near, but not quite close enough for me to touch. I swirled a hand in the pool. She followed the motion of my fingers. I traced a pattern beneath the surface and used my power to draw the smoothed gray and black pebbles on the bottom of the pool into a swirling dance with the water.

She gasped, a petite sound, almost inaudible, but her voice wrapped around my heart. My mate, for her mere presence convinced me she was the one woman destined for me. The longed for fated mate all Fae desired and not a choice of duty for the sake of our people. There would never be another woman for me now I'd located my true intended. I leaned closer to the edge of the cobalt pool. A surge of satisfaction pounded deep inside. I didn't flaunt my immense royal powers over all the elements in the presence of the other Fae. It was enough being a royal without the added reminder I was so much more different to them. They didn't need to see them on display. Besides, my swirling crown gave away who and what I was, but my powers raged to be free in front of this Fae woman.

I slid my hand out of the water and called vines to creep across the cobblestones to tickle the soles of her feet. She smothered a laugh with her hand, but her chest shook. Dia, she enchanted me with her mirth. With another wave of my ability, the vines burst into flowers the same hue as her eyes. She brushed a hesitant finger over a bloom. The stroke of her touch caressed the depths of my very being.

I cocked my head, studying the daintiness of her feet and the delicate lines of her slim ankles where they disappeared under the silky length of her gown. My imagination ran amok, sending eager ideas of my power stroking her legs to watch her squirm with passion. I flung the vines away with frustration. I wouldn't take this beautiful creature here as much as I longed to. As much as I wanted to hear her say she was my mate too. I couldn't make her mine, not while my party reverberated throughout the palace.

This woman deserved more than I could give her at this moment.

A night with a prince might be some Fae women's desire, but I sensed with every ounce of my being that this woman didn't want a moment of ecstasy with a royal. Tonight was the night I needed to choose a mate, and I'd chosen. At two hundred years old, it was time I put the royal family and the Fae race first. I'd promised my parents, the King and Queen of the Fae, I'd do everything in my power to produce more heirs to the throne. A mate was the one to do that. This woman who wouldn't even speak to me was my fated mate. I wouldn't need to choose one of the other high-pitched Fae women to spend eternity with.

My powers swirled the air into a breeze and blew her soft curls from her shoulders. Goosebumps rippled across her flesh. She must be mine. If she'd talk to me, we could start our lives together and get to know one and other before we placed our claiming marks.

If she'd give me something simple like her name as a start.

"What is your name?"

She jerked to a stand. The floaty material of her sleeves appeared as though she possessed wings, the illusion amplified as she spun and fled the atrium as fast as her bare feet would take her.

I let her flee. A smile tugged the corners of my lips. She wouldn't get far.

CHAPTER THREE
NIAMH

MY HEART RACED ALONG with the speed of my feet through the marble halls. *What were my parents thinking about agreeing to me coming here tonight?*

The Prince was intimidating. Powerful. Electric. And so handsome. His silver locks hung to his sharp jaw, brushing against the corners of his kissable red lips. His mesmerizing blue and indigo eyes had enthralled me. Mother's words rang in my ears. She'd be happy to know the rumors were true. The Prince was stunning. To experience his attraction firsthand had rendered me speechless. A good thing too, since one little song note from me around men caused complications. The sip of the spring's water, while powerful, may not have helped my predicament. I didn't want the first man I tried it on to be the Prince.

He'd asked me to call him Fintan, not Prince or Prince Fintan. Somehow his name made our time together intimate. I longed to roll his name off my tongue, but the influence of my voice would trick him into believing I was his mate as so many other men before him decreed. Especially if I slipped one song note into my speech, which sometimes happened when I was nervous or excited. A hollow laugh spluttered past my lips. Ironic I wanted to kiss him when I'd never wanted to kiss any man. It was the unexpected desire that sent me running from the atrium, for I had nothing to offer any man, least of all a prince. Not that he'd want me. The daughter of a brewer and a singer from a remote Fae settlement on Earth—a place the Royals seldom visited. After seeing the elegant beauty of the Summer Court for myself for the first time, I didn't blame them.

But tonight was my only night here. Tonight, I'd sing for the Royal Court, for the Prince's two hundredth birthday party, and for the night he'd choose a mate. As much as I loved singing, I hated the effect of my voice on men. I wanted the simple pleasure of entertaining people and sharing my love of songs. I'd do anything to get rid of the lure my voice evoked in so many men.

Pain lanced my heart, and I slammed into the crystal wall with a loud slap of my palms.

How would I sing for the Prince to find his mate when my heart hurt so?

I struggled to breathe. My limbs weakened. Using the wall as support, I continued to the grand ballroom under the sweeping white quartz arches. I clung to the velvety yellow curtains and paused, taking one slow breath after another, focusing on the beauty of the room instead of the people inside it. The chandeliers hung from the tall ceiling many feet high. Their candles flickered around the wrought gold, making the goldstone floor underneath shine even brighter. So much grander than our humble home on Earth. The power in the stones settled the shaking in my legs, and the pain in my heart eased into a dull ache.

With my breathing back to normal, I made my way through the guests dressed in graceful gowns and robes. All the Fae in the Summer Court appeared to be in attendance tonight. *Why wouldn't they?* A chance to mate with a prince was a rare occurrence.

At the end of the grand ballroom, the King's royal aide, Grieg, waited, his face set in a passive mask. He held his arm out and escorted me onto the stage. I'd never sung in front of this many Fae. Everyone in our family and surrounding villages told me I was talented, and my singing was impressive, but I trembled with nerves before the enormous crowd because the Prince would hear my voice. He'd hear the allure of my singing and, like so many other men, he'd believe me to be his mate. I didn't want him to succumb to the seduction of my singing. For a moment longer, I wanted to live in the minuscule fantasy where Fintan could be mine for real.

Grieg clapped his hands with a loud boom, shattering my fantasy. All sound ceased in the ballroom and every face turned my way. I searched the crowd for the Prince, whose face captured my attention, and perhaps a small part of my heart. I shook the notion aside. Ludicrous. I couldn't give a piece of my heart to a man I didn't know. But my heart agreed with my earlier thought. The Prince strolled through the archway I'd entered from. He flicked his robe back with a regal air. The crowd parted for his path across the ballroom.

"Ladies and Gentlemen," Grieg boomed, "we have the esteemed privilege of presenting to you the youngest singer and songwriter amongst our people, Niamh O'Keeffe."

Prince Fintan swung to face the stage. Our gazes met. His lips spread into a grin. His look alone sent a quiver of desire through my body.

A round of applause broke out amongst the crowd, breaking the spell. I curtsied and strode to the center of the stage. A flare of power exploded and a white light landed on my face. I scanned the throng of Fae for the instigator, but the light shone too brightly for me to make out anyone's face, let alone the handsome face of the Prince.

I wet my lips and opened my mouth.

Once we were a walking,
The shadows were a talking,
The sun she was a missing,
So early in the morning.
Our love was building, building,
Our love was growing, growing,
Our love was never-ending.
Twice we were a touching,
The hands were a petting,
The fingers were a stroking,

So late in the afternoon.
Our love was building, building,
Our love was growing, growing,
Our love was never-ending.
Thrice we were a kissing,
The lips were a caressing,
The fires were a building,
So early in the evening.
Our love was building, building,
Our love was growing, growing,
Our love was never-ending.
Once, twice, thrice, our bodies were quaking.
Once, twice, thrice, our limbs were shaking.
Once, twice, thrice, our pleasures were exploding.
Once, twice, thrice, our passions were rekindling.
Our love,
Our love,
Our love never-ending.

Another round of applause swelled across the ballroom so loud my ears rang. My body warmed with the praise. This was all I'd ever wanted, to be applauded for my songs and singing. But the uncertainty of the lure in my voice sent my stomach into a hard knot. I'd sung in the presence of the royal family, in front of a large crowd, and performed an original song. My heart pounded for a different reason.

Did the Prince sense the influence in my voice? Did I bewitch him into believing I was his?

The harp behind me chimed. I flicked a nod at the harpist and stepped from the stage. I would sing again tonight after others performed for the many guests and the Fae Royals.

"Well, Niamh, at least I know your name now," Prince Fintan said.

He stepped in front of me, leaned forward, and brushed his lips across my cheek.

"Pleased to make your official acquaintance."

A tingle of awareness exploded from the place he touched.

"The pleasure is mine, Prince Fintan." I curtsied.

"Not yet." He cocked a thick eyebrow. "Perhaps by the end of the night it will be."

My cheeks warmed. "No, thank you."

CHAPTER FOUR
FINTAN

THE LITTLE VIXEN RACED across the expanse of the ballroom so fast she was a blur of flying lilac. I stalked after her. There was no way I'd let her go this time. I'd been certain she was my fated mate in the atrium, but now I'd heard her sing. Dia, there wasn't a single doubt in my mind this woman and I were meant to be together. Her voice had hit me with the intensity of a thousand Fae Royals, and almost brought me to my knees on the ballroom's floor.

That would have caused a ruckus.

Instead, I gripped the tiny blue and white flower she'd stroked in my hand with forced gentleness so I didn't crush the bloom.

"Not so fast this time, Niamh." I caught up to her at the edge of the ballroom, away from the crowd, and placed my palm on her shoulder.

She spun with a flash of her blue moonstone eyes and a flutter of dark lashes, so at odds with her silvery-yellow hair.

"Please don't do this," she whispered.

Her gaze dropped to my hand as though I hurt her, but my touch was lighter than a feather. Niamh's chest heaved in the confines of the bodice. I wanted to rip the fabric away with my teeth. Or power. Whichever would satisfy her the most.

"I have to," I said, shifting closer to my mate until the fullness of her skirts brushed against my legs. "You're mine."

"Not possible."

She firmed her pink lips—lips I craved to ravish and tease. Lips I longed to experience on my raging body.

"It is." I stroked my hands down the back of her arms.

She stepped forward, away from my touch, but ended up plastered to my front.

"Oh, Dia," she muttered.

"Oh, Dia, indeed," I whispered. "Don't you sense our connection?"

Her gaze landed on my lips. Desire burned under her dark lashes, but then those stunning blue eyes lifted to my crown of modest thorns and hardened to ice.

"No." She pushed out of my arms. "No. It's the power of my voice compelling you. Other men have said the same and 'tis not been true. You're meant for a woman of grace, of stature, of..." She waved her hand at the crowded room.

"I don't want them. I want you."

"You can't have me. I'm nothing." She raised both hands to her chest, covering the heaving of her breath as much as she could. But I noticed the telltale sign and the way her words hurt her more than me.

"You are something." I folded my arms over my chest so I wouldn't drag her into my embrace where she belonged. "You're an amazing singer and songwriter. Your words are powerful, meaningful, and desirable."

"You want me because of the power in my voice and because I sang about sex."

"You sang about love," I said.

"I sang about sex, which I know nothing about. Love either."

"You've never had sex?" I gaped at the exquisite woman. *What man wouldn't want to have sex with her?*

Niamh shook her head, sending her curls bouncing over her bare shoulders.

"Dia." I rubbed my face. "How old are you?"

"Fifty."

"You're still young in years for a Fae. No wonder you haven't experienced sex."

She placed her hands on her hips, leaving her cleavage on delicious display. "I'm not young. I've received many offers and refused them all, as I have with the mate claims."

"Their claims were false." I waved my hand, unconcerned with her reference to other men wanting to claim her. Of course, she wouldn't accept when they weren't her mate because *I was*. Inconceivable I'd been about to choose someone who wasn't mine just for the sake of the kingdom. "How can you be my mate when you're so young?"

"I'm not." She spun with a huff and stormed back to the stage on the other side of the ballroom.

Grieg, the royal announcer, introduced her again with his booming voice. A round of applause echoed through the ballroom, setting my hackles on the rise.

If what she said was true, how many men in here believed she was their mate from the power in her voice?

My power swirled. *'I'm not.'* Her words rang in my ears over and over.

How could she deny what we were meant to be? How did she not recognize the signs of a fated mate? The burning pulse of our power intent on marking each other, to share our minds and bodies.

Niamh's powerful voice drifted from the stage; strong, yet delicate, and beautiful, like her.

Is she right? Is her voice making me want her as my mate?

Oh, Prince, oh Prince, you must remember,
Your place and your power.
Oh, Prince, oh Prince, you must confess,
Your heart beats for another.
For in your life, 'tis better to make your stand elsewhere.
For in your position, 'tis a princess you need by your side.
Oh, Prince of the Summer Court,
Your beauty astounds us all,

But one will love you.
She will hold you.
She will be the princess for you.
Oh, prince of power,
Prince of beauty,
Prince of all life provides.
Royalty is in your blood,
Therefore, you mustn't decide.
Your life is here.
Your love is here.
Your crown must bear your heart.
A prince without a crown,
Is nothing but a spirit
Of what could have been,
Of the greatness lost,
Of a future king.
Oh, Prince, your princess, she awaits you
In this very court.

Did she make up the song on the spur of the moment to convince me she wasn't my mate? How talented is she? As the last notes of her lyrics trickled to an end, I found myself not liking the strength and intensity in her voice, nor the lyrics she'd sung to me on purpose. She may as well have stabbed me through the heart with the sharpness of her words.

I stalked to the refreshment table and flung back a glass of peach and apple cider. The Summer Court's intoxicating brewed fruit burned down my throat the way her words burned my heart.

Who did she think she was to deny my claim?

Father glided across the floor of the ballroom through the mass of Fae, ignoring them as he headed straight toward me. I scooped my cup into the crystal bowl and flung back another drink.

"Son." Father nodded, his prominent swirling crown of thorns rustling in his white hair.

"Father." I nodded back, my lesser crown eddied in response to his power.

He filled a cup and sipped at the liquid. "Do you have something to tell me?"

"Not a thing."

He grunted. "I'm not a fool. You desire the singer."

"Aye," I admitted. There was no point denying what my father saw for himself.

"And she desires you."

I dropped my cup on the table with a clatter. "No."

"There is something about her I can't figure out."

"Such as?" The possibility she was my mate. A woman with a rare Fae power in her voice if I believed what she said. I needed to be certain her words weren't true before I declared I'd found my fated mate.

He righted my cup and set his down next to it. "I'll figure it out by the end of the night."

Mother tilted her head at us. A bunch of women tittered around her. She waved us over. I stifled a sigh at listening to more inane giggles.

Father inclined his head at Mother. "Tonight is about finding you a mate. Go find her."

My power wanted Niamh. I desired her with every breath I inhaled. I'd already found my mate, but duty to the royal family, to all the guests, and the hopeful Fae women forced my legs to walk toward the giggling women. The burning need to protect Niamh from anyone and everyone gathered the power in my palms. Including protecting her from the King until I could convince Niamh to accept she was meant for me and I was hers.

CHAPTER FIVE
NIAMH

PRINCE FINTAN DANCED WITH Fae woman after Fae woman dressed in stunning gowns decorated in glittering threads, beads, and lace. Each woman was more beautiful and refined than the last. I wanted to slash them down with one of our farm sickles. Many men gazed at me with longing, but not one ventured close, not like they usually did when I performed. I assumed their hesitation was from the tall, imposing Fae guard clothed in red following my every step. I couldn't fault the Prince for protecting me from unwanted declarations of mating. But he didn't glance my way. He may as well kick me in the stomach for the pain rippling through me whenever he was in another woman's arms.

What did I expect? I'd denied our attraction. I'd denied his claim that I was his mate. He'd moved on to find a new mate, and I'd head home to Earth in another day and leave the splendor of the Summer

Court. I lifted my chin. It wasn't every day a farm girl like me performed in the royal palace. I'd absorb every detail of the Fae Kingdom while here since they'd made me come, like the magnificence of the palace, and the serenity of nature so similar but different to Earth's.

After my fourth song of the night, Prince Fintan waited for me by the stage, a smile lifting the edges of his kissable red lips.

"You have a beautiful voice, Niamh."

I wrenched my gaze away from his mouth. "Why are you here?"

"To ask you to dance, of course." He held out his arm with a flourishing twirl.

The arm other women held while he danced with them. The pain was intense inside my chest. "Did you find your mate tonight among the many women you danced with?"

"No, she hasn't agreed to dance with me yet." He cocked his head. His smile stretched until his cheeks creased with lines. "Ah, my mate is jealous."

"I am not." I shouldn't be jealous when he wasn't mine, but I was. Still, I placed my hand on his arm to cover the stutter of my words. A jolt of power surged from my palm through the material of his suit.

The Prince laughed and drew me onto the dance floor. "Your lies grow feebler every time we talk."

And then we were dancing to the tunes of a flute. We skipped along with the other couples, my hand resting on his arm. My dress swished against my legs in a stream of lilac while his cloak flapped behind him in a gold stream. We danced circles around each other with no contact, but the power between us simmered and our gazes locked with intensity. Then we were touching again and our palms warmed against the other's. The flute player finished the song, and the Prince dipped a bow while I curtsied. I didn't want our dance to end. Having Fintan to myself for a dance was the best moment of my life.

"Thank you for the dance, Prince Fintan." I stepped backward before I asked him to dance with me again.

"Fintan," he said. "My mate should call me by my name."

I shook my head. "I'm not."

He sighed. "How many dances do I require to convince you?"

"Dances won't convince me I'm your mate."

"No?" He raised a thick eyebrow. "You're right, dances won't suffice. Come, let me show you something." He flourished his arm in invitation again.

"If you show me this one thing and I'm still not convinced, will you admit it's the power in my voice affecting you?"

He frowned, then smiled. "Agreed."

I stepped forward and placed my palm on his arm. Warmth and power zinged between our bodies. I'd never experienced this heat and power surge from a man. A small part of me wondered what the jolt meant.

Was there a possibility he was my mate?

Prince Fintan led me from the crowded ballroom and outside into the inky darkness of the night. He unbuttoned his cloak and draped the thick fabric over my shoulders.

"You're aware we Fae do not suffer from the coolness of night?"

He chuckled. "Yes. Wear my cloak anyway, it makes me feel better."

"Better in what way?"

He rolled his broad shoulders in a shrug. "Tell me something about yourself."

"What?" I asked with hesitation.

"Anything. I want to learn all about you."

He placed his palm on the small of my back.

"If you're my mate, as you claim, then when we mark each other you'll have access to my memories."

He eased the pressure of his hand. "Humor me, Niamh."

I sighed. "I grew up on Earth. This is my first time at the Summer Court."

"Astounding."

He paused and faced me.

"What do you think so far?"

"It's magnificent. So much prettier than Earth."

"I love it here," he said. "The weather on Earth is so up and down. Here is constant."

"Yes, that's a good way to describe it."

We resumed walking and eased closer with every step we took, but it wasn't enough. The heat of his body called to me and I longed to be nearer still. I blinked away the attraction of Fintan.

"Where are we going?" I asked.

"Nowhere and everywhere," he said.

"How will you show me this one thing to convince me if we're to travel nowhere and everywhere?"

"Because I am the one thing."

I scoffed, about to tell him he was wasting his time, but he waved his hands, and all around us small golden lights lit up the woods. Thousands upon thousands of fireflies flittered through the trees.

"Oh," I gasped.

"Dance with me here."

"There's no music."

Prince Fintan flicked his hand and flaunted his shiny silver power. A nightingale's song serenaded us from the tree above. I smiled despite myself, and we repeated our dance steps from inside the grand ballroom. Out here in the enchanting lights of the fireflies and the soothing presence of the trees, the dancing was even more intimate. I curtsied, and Fintan bowed at the end of the dance. He gazed at me with such longing it was hard to not experience the same desire in his presence.

"Did you know it's the unmated male nightingale which sings at night?"

"I did not." I flicked my gaze to the trees lit up by the thousands of fireflies.

"Their nocturnal song serves to attract a mate."

"Does their singing work?"

Perhaps I shared something in common with the bird?
"Watch."

He drew me closer to the warmth of his body, turned me around, and waved his hand at the tree from which the nightingale crooned. The fireflies flew higher, lighting up the small tawny bird perched on a branch. Fintan placed his warm palms on my shoulders. His heated breath rustled the back of my hair, sending tremors rippling down my back. I was thankful for his cloak to conceal the way my body responded to his closeness. We stood with the barest of embraces for minutes, but I could have stood there for hours with the Prince believing I was his mate. Fantasies were easy in the dark of night, in the magic of the glowing fireflies and the song of the nightingale.

Another tawny nightingale landed on the branch.

"There she is," he whispered in my ear. "A mate can never resist the call of their intended."

The pair of birds fluttered around each other, the male's singing growing in happiness and volume, until the pair flew away together into the darkness of the night.

I smiled and sighed. If Fae mating was as simple as the mating of nightingales, then I might surrender to the Prince's mate claim.

But it wasn't.

Once a Fae mated, they seared a mating mark on each other's flesh with their power. They absorbed each other's memories. Gave each other their bodies. Tied themselves together forever. It could never be undone if one realized they'd chosen wrong. Or chose while under the spell of my song.

"What else do you have to show me?"

He laughed, a deep, husky timbre, setting my pulse racing. He released my shoulders and waved his hand. White daisies popped up from the ground around our feet. Fintan bent and picked the blooms, then held the bouquet out to me.

"For you, my mate."

It was too sweet to resist. I grasped the bouquet and lifted them to my chest, even though I knew I shouldn't accept them. I tipped my chin up and looked him straight in the eyes.

"You won't change my mind with flowers. I told you, it's the power in my voice making you believe I'm yours."

CHAPTER SIX
FINTAN

"**W**HAT IS THIS POWER you keep mentioning?"

I didn't understand this insistence of hers. Niamh's voice was exceptional, but her singing wasn't the reason I believed her to be mine.

"I'm not sure." She crushed the flowers tighter to her chest. "All I know is when I sing, men gaze at me with lust and stop me after my performance to declare I'm their mate."

"Have you ever believed their claims?"

"No, I felt nothing for those men." She flung her hands wide, releasing the daisies from her death grip, and sent them scattering across the ground.

"Do they listen to your denial?" Power surged into my hands, causing them to glow in the night's darkness. Every ounce of my being flared with the need to protect Niamh.

"Most do." She rubbed her palms together, the length of her sleeves fluttering with a quiet swish. "Those that don't receive a jab of my knee to their privates."

The power in my body eased until my hands no longer shone and my chest filled with pride. My mate could protect herself against unwanted claims.

I chuckled. "That would deter most men."

Niamh smiled and flicked me a look from under her dark lashes. "Would it deter you?"

"No. It would hurt." I covered my cock and balls, wincing at the reminder of the debilitating pain of taking a blow down there. "But you are my mate. You wouldn't discourage me from seeking you and easing your worries."

"Fintan."

She sighed my name like my words were breaking the hard shell of resistance she'd built around her heart.

"Is that why you drank from the spring? For the healing powers?"

Her shoulders stiffened under my cloak, and she glanced away.

"Niamh, talk to me." I threw a small amount of royal authority in my voice, even though I disliked using it.

"I hoped the spring would heal me."

"But you're not broken."

"Aren't I?" she whispered.

"No." I placed a hand on the small of her back. "You have a power. An unusual Fae power in your voice, but it is still a Fae power over nature. Just a little different."

"And your power commands all nature."

"It does." I stroked my thumb over her tight muscles. "Your power can't command men. It's not how Fae powers work."

She huffed. "Forget it."

"I won't. I'm trying to understand, but it's hard when I haven't seen it."

"You've seen it. You think I'm your mate." She stepped away from my hand.

"I *know*." I folded my arms. "Big difference."

"Not to me."

What would it take for me to convince her?

"Two hundred years, Niamh. I think I know the difference between lust and the call of my fated mate. I've never had such a struggle with my power as when I'm with you."

She snorted. "That proves nothing."

"I've never had a woman's scent fill my senses until I can't think of anything but her."

She sucked in a breath.

"I've never had my heart beat in time with another woman's, and so hard against my chest that my bones ache."

"Perhaps you are ill?" She raised an eyebrow.

"You know as well as I, Fae don't suffer from illness."

Her gaze flitted back to my face. Searching. She wouldn't find anything but sincerity in my words and actions. Her face softened as she gazed at me. I begged her with my eyes to give me a chance. Give us a chance. I'd do everything in my power to prove myself to my mate, even if she kneed me in my balls. I flourished my arm to the trail leading through the forest.

"Walk with me to the lake. I have more I'd like to show you."

CHAPTER SEVEN
NIAMH

THE PRINCE'S CHARM ENTICED me to spend more time with him, to listen to the certainty in his voice, to experience the rush in my body whenever he touched me. He bewitched me into believing we could be mates.

"I'd love to see the lake." I dipped my head.

"Do you have a family on Earth?" he asked.

"Parents, grandparents, aunts and uncles, many cousins too."

"No siblings?"

"No, no brothers or sisters."

"Like me."

"Aye." I flicked him a half-lidded look. Perhaps we weren't so different.

We fell into step over the rich loam. Fintan placed his warm palm against my lower back, sending a ripple of awareness through the small touch. I concentrated on the fireflies flickering ahead and lighting the way under the Trembling Giant trees. A gentle breeze rustled the fallen gold leaves on the ground, drifting up the length of my long dress and around my legs, teasing me with its soft touch. *Would the Prince's touch be as soft?*

"Stop," I whispered. Every second I spent with Fintan, my will to keep him at a distance crumbled a fraction further.

"Stop what?" He lifted his hands in innocence.

I slipped away from the warmth of his body and walked ahead a few steps. The breeze dropped to nothing, even though I wanted it to keep touching me. I longed for Fintan to stroke my flesh the same way his breeze traveled up my legs. My nose twitched. I missed the aroma of him. Was the allure of his scent because he was my mate? My heart raced when it had previously beat a steady rhythm next to Fintan. I slowed my steps and let him catch up with me. His palm touched my lower back again, sending my heart racing from such an innocent caress.

Snowflakes fell from the dark sky amongst the fireflies, light, cool strokes over my heated cheeks. I brushed one, then two, away. Fintan may as well have been using his lips. A shiver of yearning drifted from my face and lower until I almost asked him to kiss me so I could experience the rapture of this new desire.

The snowflakes stopped. I heaved a deep breath to calm my racing heart. We stepped through the lush grass around the gleaming water of the lake. The sun broke across the horizon in a display of burned orange and bold pink and reflected against the water.

"It's so beautiful," I gasped.

"Nothing is as beautiful as you."

The water rose into a pattern of jets reflecting the colors of sunrise and landed with ripples of bright yellow, creating more patterns on the surface.

"You can't help yourself, can you?" I faced him. A smile stretched my lips and forced my cheeks higher. His insistence at persuading me I was his mate by flaunting his powers was rather sweet. No other man had tried to convince me I was his mate. They'd just said I was and expected me to fall in line with it. No other man had made me smile the way Fintan did. I'd never wanted another man the way I wanted Fintan. Never wanted the words to be true until him.

"I can't help anything when I'm with you." He drew me to his chest, our hands trapped between us, hearts racing in time beneath our touch. "My power rages at me to be with you. To mark you as my mate in the way of the Fae."

I sucked in a sharp breath. To be marked by your mate was the ultimate of exchanges. A Fae mating mark allowed for an exchange with the other's memories in the moment of claiming. A mate would know everything about you, every secret, every past event. Fae could never undo a mating. My heart pounded and my power responded to his words, making my hands shimmer lilac in the growing light of the sunrise when they'd never shone before. My lips parted. How and why were they glowing now? Was it true? Was my power urging me to mark Fintan as my mate?

"Your power agrees with my power."

He brushed his fingers down my back. I spun away.

He eased me back to face him.

"I sensed you were mine the moment I set my eyes on you kneeling at the spring. When I touched you, my power soared for joy."

Fintan stroked my cheek with the back of his knuckles.

"Others may have wanted to claim you because of the power in your voice, but I wished to claim you before you even spoke to me. Niamh, you must sense the need to claim me for yourself. You want to press your body to mine, and feast on me with your lips. You long to know how I feel when I bury myself inside you and claim you. Don't you, my mate?"

Dia, his voice vibrated through every inch of my body. I'd never heard truer words, never felt truer words said. My throat thickened. Words wouldn't form. I couldn't agree with him. I had nothing to offer a prince except a long line of men entreating to claim me as theirs. He deserved better.

"If you won't admit we're meant to be with your words, perhaps you'll admit it with your body?" He opened my fingers and flattened my hand against his chest. "Feel my heart racing for you."

The rapid pound of his heart under my palm settled deep inside my limbs. My power longed to mark him as mine.

Is it true? Could Prince Fintan be my mate? Could the reactions he stirred inside my body be genuine?

I licked my lips. I'd never desired a man until him, and how I yearned for the pressure of his body against mine, the touch of his lips to mine.

He groaned and slid his hands to my waist, sending sparks of desire up my spine. Bit by bit, he drew me closer until our bodies rested against each other. A zing of powerful rightness coursed through my body.

"You are meant for me," he whispered.

I lifted my gaze to his. His pale blue eyes with the deep indigo rim blazed with hunger and lust, but more, a connection so deep it would sear us both. He lowered his head and brushed his lips against mine. A tentative touch. A question.

I answered with a sweep of my mouth against his. Nothing but rightness filled my heart and body whenever I was with him, and the tingles in my lips from the mere contact begged for more. I wanted this and him.

Fintan sighed. With infinite care, he brushed his lips against mine again. I pressed back and parted my lips for his. He stroked his tongue inside the tender flesh of my bottom lip. A tremble of passion shot straight to my core and made my knees buckle. He hauled me closer and kept me upright in the strength of his embrace. His tongue stroked again until my lips parted wider and his tongue sought the warm welcome of my mouth. Our lips tangled in a dance so primitive and luscious I recognized I was with my mate.

"Niamh," he sighed against my lips.

"Fintan," I sighed back.

His lips sought mine again. We kissed until neither of us comprehended the length of our lip lock. The rising of the sun into a new day shone on our connection with happiness. We parted to gaze into each other's eyes.

"Oh." I touched a trembling hand to my lips.

"Do you understand we are meant for each other now?"

I nodded. Fintan waved his hand, and the ground burst into a field of bluebonnets reaching to my waist. I brushed my fingers across the peapod-shaped flowers. With another wave of his hand, Fintan flattened a patch and urged me to sit with him. Sudden tiredness settled through my limbs. I placed a hand over my mouth to smother a yawn.

"My mate is tired." He laughed, patting his thighs. "Come rest with me."

The offer to rest my whirling head was too tempting. To take a moment and absorb the impact of his kiss. The true meaning behind it. I stretched out at an angle to him and placed my head on his lap. Surrounded by the bluebonnets, the golden sun shone onto my face. I closed my eyes. He really was the best man a woman could want for a mate, and I hardly knew him. But I wanted to.

"Tell me about being a prince."

"I don't know any different."

He smoothed a hand from the top of my head down the length of my hair to where the strands ended at my waist.

"I grew up with a loving mother and father in the palace. Father taught me how to harness my royal powers and keep them controlled."

"I wish I could control mine." I sighed.

He stroked my hair again.

"Do you think you could learn?"

"I don't think so. It's a power in our family which inflicts some women. As far as our relatives know, no one has learned how to turn off the luring call of a mate."

"Do many contain the power?"

"It happens on the rare occasion, yet here I am."

"Aye, here you are, my mate."

He stroked my hair in a soothing caress.

"My mother has amazing power over storms. She can call thunder and lightning, torrential rain, and blowing gales. She doesn't use her powers much in the Summer Court."

"I suppose not. Storms would be out of place in this utopia."

He stopped stroking my hair and laid on the crushed bluebonnets with me. I didn't stir from the comfort of his lap, fearing I'd break the spell woven around us in this moment where we were both relaxed into believing we were mates. The lulling sounds of nature crooned to us. The gentle lap of the water on the shore, the quiet chirping of birds in the forest, and the soft blow of the breeze rustling through the flowers. Never in my life had happiness and contentment filled me until this moment lying with Fintan. I drifted into sleep.

I woke with a lazy, comfortable sensation in my limbs and heart, but my head pounded with the notion this was a mistake. Believing I was really his mate. Kissing him. What would have happened if I hadn't fallen asleep? I might have let him mark me and I him. We would have tied ourselves together with no way out and all because of the lure in my singing.

A chill blew across the lake, sending a shiver of unease through my body even, with his cloak wrapped around me. I sat up with a start. The gloom of evening had set in and I gawked at the man I'd fallen asleep with. Fintan. The Prince.

What a night and day. My first kiss. My lips still vibrated from the intensity of our connection.

But what if his feelings weren't real? What if my feelings were mine alone?

Fintan's silver lashes lay against his pale cheeks. His face was soft in slumber. His red lips parted, almost begging me to kiss him awake. And I wanted to. Wanted to experience his lips on mine again and again. Maybe even for the rest of my life. I tucked my nose into his cloak and inhaled his scent.

But this was just a silly daydream. I was never any man's true mate.

I flung his cloak from my shoulders and stood with a start for I shouldn't and couldn't have him as my mine.

How would I ever be useful as the prince's mate and a member of the royal family when all I ever did was lure men into believing they were my mate? I had nothing to offer. He'd spend the rest of his life fighting for me. And he'd get hurt like my father. I couldn't have that. He deserved so much better.

Besides, the power in my voice must have tricked him, and he wasn't really mine. I pushed through the flowers and raced into the forest. Away from the one man who could change my mind if he was awake. He'd changed it once, and I knew he would only have to utter one word and he'd change it again. I was doing this to protect him from making a terrible mistake. He'd realize that as soon as I wasn't near him. The lure from my song wouldn't last and he'd find a mate who was worthy of him, who'd give him what I could never give. A life of peace.

My footsteps felt like they thudded so loud I was sure to wake him. Maybe it was the pounding of my heart? I ran into the forest and weaved through the giant trees. A red shadow stepped onto the path. I skidded to a stop at the imposing sight of the royal aide.

"Niamh, I have been looking for you," Grieg said. "'Tis time for me to escort you to your next performance."

I frowned. "The Prince's Ball is over."

"Aye, but King Diarmuid received a request for all the ball's performers to attend the Water Sprite's Ball tonight."

"I can't." I shook my head with a savage twist of my neck.

"It's a royal decree." His lips thinned.

"I have no choice again?"

He waved his hand, sending a surge of his power to open the veil rippled in a claret red curtain.

Shite. Not again. How many men would I ensnare this time?

"What are the Water Sprites like?" I asked.

"You've never met one?"

"No." I ducked my head. "I'm a simple farm girl."

He offered me his arm. I stared at it for a few beats of my heart before placing my hand on the sleeve of his red coat. There was no zing of rightness like when I'd placed my hand on Fintan. I glanced back the way I'd left the Prince sleeping. Unaware I was about to leave the Summer Court. To the place we'd connected. The place I'd experienced my first kiss. My lips hungered for more of his kisses. I touched a trembling finger to my mouth. One perfect kiss from Fintan would have to last me a lifetime of loneliness.

"It's not my place to say," Grieg said, escorting me through the veil. "I just do what I'm told."

Him and me both apparently.

CHAPTER EIGHT
FINTAN

F ROM THE MOMENT CONSCIOUSNESS returned, I sensed Niamh had left the Summer Court. I curled a fist on my chest over the ferocious pain stabbing my heart. Her softness and quiet, even breaths had lulled me to sleep with her when I should have marked her instead. If I had, then I could track her with the strength of our mating mark. Now, I had to find her on Earth, and that world was substantial. I fisted the flowers and ripped them from the soil. A growl rumbled deep in my throat. A precise location of Niamh would work better before I separated the veil.

"Feck."

Birds scattered from the treetops.

How would I find her?

Wait. We'd invited her to perform at my birthday ball. Father would have sent a royal decree to her home. The Fae King would possess the information I needed.

With a swipe of my hand, the bluebonnets vanished, just like my mate did. I sprinted across the open expanse of the field, through the Trembling Giant forest, and along the path up to the glittering crystal palace. The power surging in my body flung open the white oak front door.

"Father," I bellowed.

Grieg appeared. "They're in the great hall."

I stormed through the marble hallways and into the great hall, growing more desperate to find Niamh the longer I was away from her. Mother and Father looked up from the grandiose long granite table perched on their throne-like chairs.

"How do I find her?" I demanded.

"Who?" Father put his cup on the table.

"Sit down, my son, eat with us." Mother waved at the chair beside her.

"I don't have time to eat," I snapped.

Mother's eyes narrowed. Her hands glowed. A small spark of lightning flashed in the air above my head.

"Sit," she commanded. "Tell me why you are so riled up?"

I jerked out a chair and sat with a thud. There was no use avoiding my mother's demands, in particular when feeding her son. She piled a helping of fresh fruit and soft pieces of bread onto my plate from the platters on the table. Not that I could stomach food right now. I'd tell her that, but she'd probably zap my ass with lightning.

"Who are you looking for?" she asked.

"The woman, Niamh O'Keefe. She sang at my party last night."

"Ah, yes, the dainty creature with the voice of a nightingale. Why are you looking for the singer?" Mother asked.

"She's my mate. I need to find her."

Father tilted his head. "She's your mate? You realize her voice has the power of seduction?"

"She said the same thing, but I don't hear it. All I hear is her, all I see is her, and when we touch, all I feel is her. Niamh is mine."

"How lovely," Mother said. "I'm happy you found your mate."

Father steepled his fingers and rested his chin on them. "You are certain?"

"As certain as the royal power coursing through my veins."

"I'm not convinced. You're a royal, with royal obligations. You need a suitable mate, one who will stand by your side and not seduce men with her voice."

"Father." I shoved back my chair. "I've seen the difference between a fated mate and a chosen mate. You wanted me to choose a mate, and I did. You won't change my mind. Besides, you can't change destiny. I will mark Niamh as mine and she will mark me and there's nothing you can say that will stop that from happening."

The King rose from his chair with a slowness that let me know he battled with his powers. I understood his battle. My own raged inside me, eager to remove anyone who stood between me and my mate. Father or not. King or not.

Mother produced a rumble of thunder. Inside the palace.

"Sorry, Mother." I dropped my head.

"But..." Father said.

Another crack of thunder exploded.

"Very well." Father sighed. "She returned to Earth to sing at the Water Sprites' masquerade ball this very night. Sir Axis insisted all our performers at your ball would entertain at his too." He raised his eyes to the ceiling. "I couldn't say no without undue cause. You know the power they possess could end us all."

I swallowed. "The masquerade ball where the sprites choose their harems or add to them?"

"Yes, the very ball."

"Why would you do that?" I bit out. "Especially when you realized her voice seduces men?"

"I wasn't certain until you said she was your mate. She's probably bewitched you too."

"Her voice isn't why I think she's mine," I ground out through clenched teeth. "Did you not hear a word I said?"

"I did." He ran a hand over his crown. The swirling thorns settled under his touch.

I shook my head. Father might never believe it. But I did.

"Shite, I need to go. Niamh is young and innocent. She probably doesn't even know the intricacies of Water Sprites. She could be in danger."

"If she's your mate, you have nothing to worry about," Mother said. "Sir Axis wouldn't let any harm come to a guest at his ball. Let alone a Fae."

"Mother, you know the sprite's reputation as well as I do. Do you believe they'd allow her to leave if the power in her voice seduces the sprites?"

"Well, I suppose not, if you haven't marked her as your mate."

"I have not." I waved my hand and separated the veil in a shimmering display of rippling silver-white energy. "I intend to fix that as soon as I fetch my mate home."

"Wait." Mother slid her chair back and picked up a mask from the table beside her. "You'll need this for the ball."

I raised both eyebrows.

How did I miss the extravagant mask beside her?

"You knew this would happen."

She raised the black mask to my face and tied the ribbons behind my head.

"I noticed how besotted you were last night, and I hoped you'd win her over, but as mothers do, I prepared for all contingencies." She shot Father a look. "Your father has his doubts, but he has your best interests in mind."

She patted my cheek.

"I, no, we, believe in you."

I kissed her cheek with the love I held for my thoughtful mother and stepped through the shimmering silver-white veil. My thoughts focused on the Water Sprites' territory on Earth and I exited the Summer

Court into the luminous blue of a grand ballroom. The sprites had set an abundance of round tables with pink roses and glowing candles. They filled the chairs dressed in barely there clothes, eating, talking, flirting, kissing. I searched the masked faces. Niamh was nowhere to be found amongst the tables. I scooted around the edge of the ballroom, not wanting to draw attention to myself unless it was necessary since I was here without an invitation. The musicians on the stage tweaked their instruments, soft drumming, a twang of a viola, and more, before flowing into a song. Sprites streamed onto the dance floor, swaying to the sensual tunes. Then the voice I craved to hear carried over the top of the music.

Niamh was resplendent in a pale blue gown the same color as her eyes. I glided closer to the stage, enthralled by my mate and her melodious singing words of love. Her voice was beautiful as always, just as she was, but there was a tenseness to the curve of her neck and bare shoulders I didn't fail to notice. Did she not want to be here? Did she still want to be by my side?

A few sprites joined me beneath the stage and gazed at Niamh with wonder, lust, and enchantment flashing across their faces. The spell of her voice. I saw the allure in her song now, surrounded by the Water Sprites. Last night, I wasn't certain about the influence in her voice causing others to think she was theirs, but these sprites wanted her with an obsession that glowed in their lust-filled eyes.

A rumbling growl rolled through my chest. The Water Sprites swung their gaze from Niamh to me. I bared my teeth and lifted my hands, now glowing with power and sending crackling energy through the air.

"She's mine," I roared.

Power swirled up my robes, whipping them in a flurry of tornado. I flicked my fingers and, taking a leaf out of my mother's book, I sent multiple blasts of lightning to the ground. Indigo and violet sparks exploded, throwing the Water Sprites to the edges of the ballroom. The musicians ceased playing their instruments and scuttled to the back of the stage. Niamh stopped singing, eyes wide under the intricate blue mask twined around her delicate face.

"Prince Fintan, what is the meaning of this?" The Water Sprites Master, Sir Axis Foxlace, strode onto the dancefloor. "You come into my territory, my party, and threaten my people?"

"Apologies, Sir Foxlace, but this Fae woman is my mate."

"Your mate?" His blue eyes blazed. "Have you marked her, young prince?"

I hesitated.

He laughed. "She's fair game then."

Someone tossed him a glowing blue sword.

I clapped my hands and called a matching water sword into my palm.

Axis lunged and swung at my head. I ducked and narrowly avoided losing my brains. He charged with a smirk etched on his face. I raised my sword and blocked his blow. Our swords met with a clang and flash of blue sparks, sending the force vibrating through my hand

and up my arm. We parried stroke for stroke. Advances, blocks, retreats. Our swords ripped through the air with loud swishes and near misses. We danced around the floor, neither of us going for the kill shot, more a testing of each other's sword skills.

Axis swung at my feet. I jumped over his sword. I could end this now with all my powers, but I wouldn't do anything further to make the Water Sprites think about attacking us. Although I'd probably done enough of that tonight with my lightning strikes. But Niamh was mine, and I'd fight for her. My lips twitched into a small smile. Dia, how I'd battle for her. I lunged and the tip of my sword slashed across his side. Blue blood welled atop his tanned skin. An answering smirk stretched his lips to bare his teeth, as though he realized I'd had enough with our testing session. He returned my lunge for one of his own. The tip of his sword caught my cheek. I didn't feel the pain. My adrenalin surged. Protect my mate. I wouldn't let anyone get their hands on Niamh.

I wiped away the blood on my cheek. The cut had already healed.

"Stop," Niamh yelled.

Niamh's voice blasted across the dance floor, along with a surge of lilac power from her hands. So strong was her power, the air rippled. It sent us flying to land on the floor with a loud back cracking thud and clatter of our swords as it cast them from our hands and skittered across the floor.

I recovered before Axis and lunged to my feet.

Axis shook his head. "What was that?"

"My mate." I smiled.

"She did that?" He raised an eyebrow. "And she's your mate?"

"Aye. Niamh's previous engagement at your masquerade ball interrupted our courtship," I said. "I wouldn't have caused a scene if your subjects didn't want to claim what is mine."

"I see," Axis said, running his gaze over Niamh. Assessing. Calculating.

My power bristled again. I still wanted to slice him to pieces for getting between me and my mate.

Niamh studied him back from the stage. Her wide gaze dipped from his bare, tanned, muscular chest to the tightness of his leather pants. Even under the luminescent blue lights, her cheeks tinged with pink. *Adorable.*

"Miss O'Keeffe, what do you have to say in this matter? Is Prince Fintan here your mate, or are these sprites salivating at your feet your mates?" Axis strode to the edge of the stage.

Niamh's throat worked as she swallowed over and over. She lifted a hand to her chest, covering the heaving of her lungs.

"Niamh." I stepped to the bottom of the stage and stood at her feet. "Tell the truth. That's all you need to do. No one will make you say or do anything you don't want to."

"He's right, pretty songbird," Axis said. "Speak freely without fear of reprisal."

She tapped her fingers on her forehead. "Up here I'm uncertain who is my mate." She tapped her fingers on her chest above her heart. "Here I'm convinced that Fintan is mine."

Axis smirked, his gleaming white teeth glowing blue under the luminous lights. "Pretty songbird, listen to your heart. Now, do you wish to leave the ball with Prince Fintan as his mate, or stay and sing, perhaps join a harem here as a mate?"

Niamh's gaze flitted to the crowd of Water Sprites scattered around the edges of the ballroom. A few stared, still enthralled with the power in her voice, and longing to include her in their harems.

What man wouldn't?

She was exquisite. If she didn't leave soon, Niamh would see how much the Water Sprites wanted her. Then she'd experience more than one lover if that's what she desired and have to share any lover she chose with others. As if my thought transferred into her mind, she strode from the stage and to my side. She slid her hand into mine. The instant connection with my mate made my power grow brighter. Niamh's power responded in kind and merged with the glow of mine in a dazzling display of silvery indigo.

"I'll leave with my mate, Prince Fintan. Thank you for inviting me to sing at your ball, Sir Foxlace." Niamh curtsied with a swish of her silk gown.

Axis stepped closer and bowed, his long dark hair falling over his bare chest. "The pleasure was all ours, sweet Niamh. You're welcome to perform for my people any time you wish. Now we know of your intended mating, my subjects won't step out of line again."

The sight of a half-dressed man so close to my unmarked mate sent my power thrumming, but I forced the urge down. The master water sprite straightened. A smirk kicked up the corner of his lips, but he said nothing as the musicians struck up a tune. In answer, the sprites stepped onto the dance floor and swayed together in a sensual rhythm of limbs. I hauled Niamh to my side, wrapped an arm around her waist, and parted the veil in a shimmering silver-white haze.

We left the masquerade ball and Earth for the great hall in the Summer Court palace. Mother and Father glanced up from the dining table. I ripped the mask from my face, untied Niamh's dainty blue mask and tossed them on the floor. I didn't want any reminder of the masquerade ball and how Niamh might have ended up in a Water Sprite harem.

"You're back already." Mother stood. She swept toward us in her plum-colored gown and kissed Niamh's cheeks in welcome. "You must be my son's mate."

"I, uh," Niamh said.

Father joined Mother's side. "You're uncertain because of your power."

"I am." She nodded.

"Good. This power in your voice is unusual. I can't have my son mating with a Fae I am unsure about," Father said.

"Father," I growled, stepping in front of Niamh. "Niamh is not trying to trick me."

"How can we be sure? We know nothing about her or her family. They live on Earth and don't visit the Summer Court. That is strange."

"A few in my family have married humans," Niamh said.

Father scowled. "Marked mates are always welcome in the Summer Court."

I huffed out a breath. "Fae can't mark humans, you know that, Father."

No wonder Niamh's family didn't come to the Summer Court when they'd have to leave some of their loved ones behind.

"Diarmuid, stop this nonsense." Mother placed her hand on his chest. "I won't have you driving our son and his mate away. Fintan has chosen his mate. We need to respect that. There must be a way we can put everyone's minds at ease."

Father slid his hand over Mother's and gazed into her eyes. "There might be a way we can settle this."

"How?" Niamh and I said at the same time.

Father clucked his tongue. "You should always come to your King with your problems or your father." He zeroed his gaze on me. "We'll visit the royal aide witch, Saltine Woodswillow."

CHAPTER NINE
NIAMH

THE FAE KING PARTED the veil to Earth in a dazzling display of rainbow colors so different from the silver-white of Fintan's power. We traveled from the Summer Court to a weeping willow forest alongside a running brook on Earth and walked a narrow dirt path. The branches of the willows hung with slender leaves and stretched out as though attempting to touch us. A shiver ran down my spine, even with Fintan's warm palm on the small of my back. At the end of the path sat a white house with a dark thatched roof and tall pointed arches. A small gray stone knee-high wall surrounded the residence with a tiny timber gate.

A witch dressed in a long black gown opened the front door.

"Ah, your majesty." She dipped her head. "What brings you to my humble abode?"

Her voice sent a shiver down my spine. It sounded like the eerie voice in the forest.

"Saltine," he greeted, "my son and his supposed mate require your assistance."

She flowed across the cobblestone path and eyed Fintan first, then me. "Ah, I see. Come inside, young singer."

Saltine opened the timber gate. The hinges sent out a loud screech. My skin prickled. I stepped away from the warmth of Fintan's hand.

"Wait." He clutched my shoulder. "I should go with you."

"No," Saltine said. "The singer and I must do this alone."

"'Tis all right, Fintan. I need to do this." I touched my palm to his. Our powers surged with a zap and a bright flare. Fintan raised my hand to his mouth, kissed my fingers, and let go.

I followed the witch through the heavy front door into a cavernous greeting room. A black cauldron bubbled in the center of the room, alongside a dais with a leather-bound grimoire, and a long table with tiny jars of herbs and other assortments.

"Please." Saltine pointed at the cauldron.

I stepped up to the side of the cauldron big enough to fit a person. Inside, the liquid bubbled a murky brown. Saltine stood on the opposite side of me.

"Were you the voice in the forest?"

"What voice? What forest?" She flicked her hair back.

"I could have sworn it was you."

She winked. "Give me your hand."

A slight tremble ran through my limbs, but I offered her my hand over the top of the cauldron.

"You have nothing to fear. I wish to help you."

She clasped my hand in both of hers and studied the lines on my palm.

"Ah, I see, I see."

"What do you see?"

"I see a lot, young singer. You have a Siren in your family tree."

I gasped. "They are rumors from centuries ago."

"Rumors often contain an element of truth."

She brushed a finger over a line on my palm.

"Ah. Oh. You must not share this information with your mate until the time is right. The future of your people depends on it."

"So, he is my mate?"

"Well, der." She rolled her eyes. "Youngsters these days."

"Who are you?"

"Saltine."

"What are you then?"

"A bit of this and a bit of that."

She ran her finger over another line in my hand.

"Like you."

"Does the King know you're more than a witch?"

"The King knows what I tell him and nothing more. You'll keep my secrets as I'll keep yours." She narrowed her eyes. "If you want me to remove the Siren's call in your voice, that is."

"You can remove it?" My voice wobbled. "How?"

"I need a drop of your blood to make a potion to strip the Siren's power from your body. Once you drink the potion, no man will fall for the thrall of your voice again, and you'll no longer pass the curse onto your future children."

"And Fintan?"

I snapped my gaze to the knife. To no longer draw men with my song, and no longer pass this power onto female offspring and have her not suffer this uncertainty would be perfect. Even if, by stripping this power, Fintan no longer believed I was his mate, then I'd have to take the chance for my future daughter or daughters if no one else.

"You'll know the absolute truth of your mate when the Siren's call is no longer your power."

"Do it then, but won't my mate see this conversation through my memories when I mark him?"

"No, I ward my abode with a powerful protection spell. Only those inside can share the memories," Saltine said.

"Wait, I can never tell him?"

It seemed wrong to keep such a thing from Fintan. As my mate, he should understand everything there was about me, but if I was to become a prince's mate, then I needed to think like a princess. Our people were more important than one slight omission I didn't even realize was true until today.

"There will be a time, many, many moons, from now, when your mate and children will need to learn the truth. It is the only thing that will set the Fae right."

"How will I identify when the time is right?"

"You'll recognize the moment in your heart." She picked up a pointed dagger. The red ruby in the carved handle glowing like an evil eye.

"What power will I have?" My voice wobbled as the knife drew nearer.

If I didn't have the power of my voice, then what sort of Fae would I be?

"You will still have your Fae power in your voice." She twirled the dagger in midair above her palm. "You haven't noticed all you do with it, can do with it, but you will once your fear of the Siren's call is removed." The dagger stopped, hovered, the ruby shone brighter. "You'll always be different from other Fae. There's nothing I can do to change that."

I sagged with relief. I'd still be able to sing. Not just sing, but sing freely, without fear of calling men to me. "Do it then. I need to see if Fintan's feelings for me are true."

The dagger dropped into her palm. "Very well."

She pricked my finger with the tip.

A drop of blood welled on my index finger. Saltine turned my hand. My red blood fell into the bubbling cauldron. The murky brown liquid erupted into magenta and light pink smoke wafted up from the surface to coil around our joined hands. She released my fist and picked up a tiny glass vial from the table, scooped it into the liquid, and offered me the potion.

I took the vial. "What do I do with it?"

The witch cackled. "Drink it, of course."

I lifted the vial to my lips and swallowed the liquid. Pain lanced through my throat, the burning prick of a thousand needlepoints. I opened my mouth and screamed, releasing a gush of pink smoke from my mouth.

Fintan and the Fae King burst through the front door.

"What did you do to her?" Fintan demanded, wrapping his arms around me.

Saltine placed the used vial on her table. "What she wanted. Sing, little songbird, and you'll see if the brew worked."

I wiped my mouth, removing the pink smoke lingering on my lips.

"How will that prove she's Fintan's mate?" the King asked.

"The proof is in her singing." Saltine smiled, but there was nothing pleasant in it. "If the potion worked, then no other male will believe she's his mate when she sings. Only her true fated mate will, and he never needed her song to know that."

Fintan stroked his palm up my back. A thousand sparks of pleasure shot through my body. Was he mine? Truly? My body thought so.

"We'll need an audience to see if the potion worked," the King said. "We'll never know for certain unless she sings before other men."

"Agreed," I said.

"True." Saltine nodded. "You may pay me half now and the remaining half when you're certain the brew worked."

The King placed a green gemstone in the witch's hand. "Thank you for your service, Saltine."

Saltine placed the gem between her teeth and bit. "Happy to be of service, King Diarmuid."

We left without another word. Nerves churned inside my chest. What if the potion didn't work? And all my hopes and dreams shattered into a pile of cutting shards that the one man I wanted wasn't mine.

And now I was also full of secrets to keep from the King and Fintan.

CHAPTER TEN

FINTAN

NIAMH WAS ADAMANT SHE needed a crowd before she sang and I'd do anything to please my mate. Father sent a call through the Summer Court and soon the ballroom filled with eager Fae men intent on listening to Niamh sing again. I wanted to fight every single one of them and roar in their faces she was mine, but for the sake of Niamh knowing we were fated as mates, I'd let them listen.

I wanted to tell her I'd still believe she was mine no matter the outcome, but Mother swept Niamh into the sitting room with her and shut the door in Father's and my faces.

"What was that?" I asked.

Father shrugged. "Your mother putting me in my place."

He led the way to the atrium. I followed his silent order. The flowers rustled at the King's approach, and the water burbled in happiness. He paced the length of the cobblestones in the same way I had at my party.

I ran a finger over a hanging bloom.

He stopped and watched me. "You're falling for her?"

"Aye. She's sweet, and yet tough."

"Like my Orlaith. Don't let their sweetness fool you, son. Our mates have us on our knees worshipping them. As a royal, you need to show the rest of the Fae you are the leader, and your mate needs to let you do that."

"Niamh would do that."

"Are you sure? She's from Earth. She hasn't grown up with the intricacies of the Summer Court."

"Still, she regards you as the King and me the Prince. Her loyalty to the Fae isn't in question."

"And her loyalty to you?"

My blood boiled. "She'd be loyal to her mate if that's what you're asking."

"And if the potion didn't work? If many men want to claim her for themselves?"

"She's denied them all until me."

"Perhaps that is worse."

"Why?"

"She could be after the crown."

I snorted. "Niamh has no designs on the crown—unlike the many women at the ball. If you want to point fingers, look at them."

"Your eyes are clear, then?"

"My eyes are crystal clear, like our spring." I sent my power to the spring and increased the flow of water.

"Our spring is everything." He sent his power to join mine. "Without it, we'll die."

"I know, Father."

"Protecting our people is our duty."

"I know. You've drilled it into me the past two hundred years." I dropped my power.

"Good." He nodded. "One day you'll be King."

"No." My heart jolted at the idea of my father dying.

"Aye. I didn't believe my father would die either, or that I'd be King. I want you to be more prepared than me." He drew his power back until the spring bubbled again.

"You've prepared me. I'll protect the Fae with everything I have in me."

"Good, son."

He placed a hand on my shoulder.

"I'm proud of who you are and for standing up for your belief in your mate."

The warmth of his power seeped from his palm into my shoulder and traveled down my back.

"You need to wash and change clothes before Niamh's performance."

He released my shoulder.

"You wouldn't want to put her off with your smell when you claim her."

"Enough of the advice." I backed up to the archway. "I have been with enough women to know what they like."

"Aye, but being with your mate is different." He smirked.

I strode to my bedroom. Father's advice was sound. Everything should be perfect for mine and Niamh's first time. The minute she admitted we were mates, I wouldn't let anyone or anything come between us.

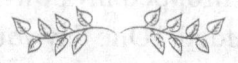

Niamh stood on the stage in her blue gown looking so regal and elegant there wasn't a doubt in my mind she was my mate. There was no chance the witch's potion destroyed the way I felt about Niamh or the way my power responded to her presence. In a constant hum, it vibrated through my hands, urging me to mark her or the beat of my heart tuning to hers when we were close.

Grieg introduced her, but his voice may well have not existed. It was my mate I longed to hear.

Niamh cleared her throat and sang.

O'er the bonny fields of bluebonnets,
The sun glowed with golden beauty,
His hand led me on a journey,
To our hearts' desires.
Through the forest of Trembling Giants,
The fireflies sparkled with light,
His hand led me on a journey,
To our hearts' desires.
By the lake of splendor,
The water danced in delight,
His hand held mine,

Our hearts beat in time.
With his hand in mine,
His lips touched mine,
My heart soared,
My body quivered,
My power responded,
Are you mine?

She didn't need to sing the song to me. I was hers. I'd always be hers, but her singing about our time together filled me with a growing love for my mate. The sort of love I wanted to spend our entire lives showering her with. First, she needed to make her way to me through the crowd of Fae. I flexed my fingers. What if the potion didn't work? What if the other men believed she was theirs? Would Niamh ever believe the conviction of my claim?

Would she ever truly be mine?

CHAPTER ELEVEN
NIAMH

T HE CROWD APPLAUDED, BUT I stayed focused on
Fintan, who'd taken the time to change clothes
while waiting for the other Fae to gather. He looked
regal in a silver outfit that blended with the silver of
his hair, eyes more vibrant and alive than ever as they
locked on me.

Did he still believe me to be his mate?

I risked a glance at the gathering of men, walked
down the steps off the stage, and paused. Fintan, King
Diarmuid, and Queen Orlaith stood at the back of the
ballroom. Even without the chandeliers lit the room
glowed with a golden hue. I curled my fingers tight,
waiting for a Fae stranger to stop me and declare I was
their mate. I took one step through the crowd. A man
bobbed his head at me. Two steps further on, another
man smiled at me. Three more and a group of men
stepped forward. I swallowed the despair building in

my mouth. My heart splintered. The potion didn't work. The pain was for nothing. Fintan would still believe me to be his, and I'd never learn if his feelings were from the Siren's call in my voice or if they were real.

My pulse pounded inside my head. I longed to return home and hide in my bedroom, say nothing of this fiasco, and shed tears for the one man I'd experienced a connection to. A man I'd love to be my mate.

"You sing beautifully," one man said. "Would you sing at my daughter's birthday?"

"Oh." I lifted a hand to my racing heart. "I'd be delighted to sing at your daughter's birthday."

"Thank you, kind lady. Shall I arrange your attendance with Prince Fintan?"

I flicked my gaze to Fintan. He'd taken a step, but the King held onto his arm, preventing him from moving any closer. He gazed at me with the same fierce protectiveness as before I drank the potion.

"Yes, you may."

Hope lifted the crushing wall from my body. I hurried across the remaining distance to Fintan. I longed to fling my arms around him, but I held back and curtsied instead.

"What did he want?" Fintan tipped his head at the man.

"He asked me to sing at his daughter's birthday."

King Diarmuid released Fintan's arm. Fintan took the last step between us, swooped me into his arms, and spun us around in a circle.

"Fintan," I squealed.

He placed me on my feet.

"Yes, my mate?"

I gasped and shoved my knuckles into my mouth.

Fintan tugged my fist away from my lips.

"You still believe I'm your mate?"

He brought my hand to his chest.

"I don't believe I'm your mate. I *know* you're mine."

He truly was mine, as I was his. The emotions I'd held in check since I met him burst free. A tear dripped from my right eye onto my cheek.

"Now, you can see? The potion worked. You'll never have to wonder ever again if my feelings for you are true. They are truer than the power coursing through my body."

He kissed the tear from my cheek.

"What do you say, mate of mine?"

I gazed into his handsome face. "I say make me yours forever."

"Come to my bedroom with me? Let me mark you in the way of the Fae?"

I nodded my head. Words were my power. My voice was my power, and Fintan now owned them as he owned me.

"A true fated mating." Queen Orlaith clapped her hands, and a bright flash of lightning struck the ground outside the palace.

"My love, control your powers." King Diarmuid clasped her glowing hands.

Her eyes sparkled like a raging storm. "I'm too overjoyed for that, darling. Perhaps we can visit Earth?"

"Aye." He parted the veil. "I know just the place for a storm."

She slid out of the King's grasp and hugged me. "When you wake from the Quiet, we'll get to know each other more."

"I'm looking forward to it." I dipped a curtsey.

"My dear, you don't curtsey now—you're a royal too."

"Except to me." The King stepped forward and held out his hand.

"Father, that is unreasonable." Fintan scowled.

"I had my reservations about this mating, but you are Fintan's fated mate, I can't argue with that," he said.

"Of course, you can't." Fintan's scowl deepened.

I placed my hand in the King's and curtsied. "I had doubts too, but I'd never do anything to hurt Fintan."

His eyebrows rose the merest of fractions before he touched a hand to my arm for a moment. "I'll hold you to that."

The King and Queen disappeared through the veil.

Grieg rushed up to us. "Where did they go?"

"To Earth," Fintan said. "Niamh and I are retiring to my bedroom to claim each other as mates. Can you please escort the guests from the ballroom?"

"Aye." Grieg bowed.

Fintan and I left the ballroom, padding through the marble halls, our footfalls a whisper on the stone. My throat thickened, unable to speak, for this moment between us was profound in so many ways. Never had I imagined my travel to the Summer Court would give me a fated mate. A prince mate too. The seduction in my voice was gone, the curse lifted from my future daughters. *Our* future daughters. Heat flooded my body at the thought of how we'd create those future children.

Fintan opened his bedroom door and drew me inside. A gentle tangling of our fingers, warmth and softness, and a hum of enticement to be closer to him still. Hand in hand, we walked toward his enormous bed surrounded by the trunks of four trees and delicate branches. Thick drapes of navy velvet hung from the corners, waiting to close us in.

"I want to mark you and I want to claim your body. I can't decide which to do first."

He released one of my hands and rubbed a palm over his face.

I lifted our joined hands to my chest, in tune with the power humming between us. I couldn't decide either. "Both."

"You're so young." He traced a finger along my collarbone. "Inexperienced."

"Teach me, mate." I tugged the ribbons loose on the back of my dress.

The front of my bodice slackened. Fintan traced a finger lower and lower until he tugged the top of my dress to my waist.

"Flawless." He lowered his head and suckled a nipple in his mouth.

Pleasure shot from my breast to my core. A raging inferno of need that simmered under my skin since the moment I met him. I yanked at the back of his robes. He shrugged out of them without releasing his mouth from my breast. My palms met warm skin. The sensation of touching my mate was so amazing. I smoothed my hands across the tight muscles in his shoulders and down his back, enjoying my first time caressing my mate.

He raised his head. "Tell me, Niamh, have you ever brought yourself to release?"

I shook my head.

"So sweet and innocent." He tugged my dress and followed it down to my feet. "I'll enjoy showing you the pleasures of your body."

He rose slowly, stroking his hands up my legs, over the curve of my hips, cupping my breasts and then my face. My mate placed his lips on mine and coaxed me into a kiss, making me mindless to everything except the masterful skill he exuded over my body. He swooped me into his arms and carried me to his enormous bed, placing me gently in the middle. Fintan stood back, his face full of desire as he stripped his pants and joined me on the soft mattress.

I stared at the enormous, straining erection between our bodies.

"Have you never seen one before?"

"No." I bit my lip.

"Dia, Niamh, maybe I should mark you first." He dropped back on the bed with a thump.

I rose over him and ran my hand down the hard length of his cock. Velveteen softness over hardness. I wrapped my fingers around him and stroked his length.

Fintan groaned. "Are you sure you've never had sex before?"

"I'm certain. I have an intense power in my chest telling me this is the right thing to do to please my mate."

He brushed my long hair behind my ears. "You could do anything and it would please me."

"Good." I placed a kiss on the top of his cock.

"Stop, my little vixen." He rolled until I was under him. "My turn to pleasure you."

"Aye." I ran my hands up his arms. "Show me."

A wicked grin stretched his lips, then he lowered them to the curve of my neck. A pleasant tingle raced across my chest. He cupped my breasts and stroked his thumbs over the hard nubs of my nipples until I longed for Fintan to suck them into the warmth of his mouth again. He followed my silent wishes at the same time his fingers met the apex of my thighs.

I jolted with so much pleasure that he flattened his other hand to my stomach and held me down while his fingers toyed with the dampness gathering in my curls. He parted my folds and found a secret spot I didn't realize existed until this moment, until him, my mate. My leg muscles tightened. Something momentous built in my body. Before the building tension broke, he slid his finger lower and breached my opening. I thrashed my head side to side, every part of my being caught up in the pleasure Fintan gave me. The slide of his finger turned my insides to a powerful pulse of carnality.

"Please," I whispered.

He captured my mouth in his and stroked his fingers in a way I didn't know was possible. He stroked until stars exploded behind my closed eyelids and the tightness in my body fluttered out in a wave of gratification that made me gasp for breath.

Fintan sat up and smiled at me. "Dia, you're exquisite."

I smiled, feeling every bit as exquisite as he'd said while I floated in the afterglow of my first orgasm.

He drew his fingers out of my damp heat and slid them into his mouth. He removed them with a loud pop. "You taste beautiful."

I giggled. "I didn't realize beauty possessed a flavor."

"Oh, it does, and it's the taste of my mate." He slid down the bed until his face was level with the place he'd just given me rapture. "I need more."

He lowered his mouth to my secret spot, not so secret now, and devoured me with his tongue. I'd believed his fingers pleased me, but his tongue licked flames of ecstasy along every nerve ending in my being. Before long, I trembled with the same tightening of muscles as before.

Fintan eased up my body and thrust his cock into the wetness he'd created. A sharp sting scorched a mark through the building pleasure. I smacked his chest with my fists. He grabbed my wrists and held them between us.

"Sorry, I should have warned you it might hurt this first time. Shh, my mate. There will only be pleasure now." He urged my clenched fists to his chest. "Come back to me, feel my heart beating for yours."

I slid my fingers open and eased my palm to his chest. My power thrummed, coating my hands.

"No, don't mark me yet. Let me give you more pleasure first." He rocked his hips.

Instead of the sharp sting of pain, a profound pleasure exploded inside my body, centered from our joining.

"More." I gasped and slid my hands to his shoulders.

"Aye, more, I'll always give you more."

He raised himself on his arms and peered down at where he'd buried himself inside me. I followed his gaze. He rolled his hips, sliding his cock along the wetness of my secret spot. *His* secret spot. I'd always be his now. Fintan rocked in a rhythm so basic and pure I had no choice but to follow it. Our breaths turned to pants. Our skin burned with heat and slicked with sweat. We lost ourselves in the perfection of two mates coming together in the primal way of all creatures.

"Niamh."

He whispered my name with reverence and stroked a finger to my hard nub down below. The rolling pleasure shattered, wave after wave of ecstasy drawing a scream from my throat.

"Beautiful, so beautiful," he whispered, and thrust into me one last time.

His body shook and deep inside my clenching muscles, a hot jet of power exploded. The pleasure took one last scream from my lungs and then we lay joined in the way of all mates bar one.

Fintan rolled over, dragging me with him until I lay over his chest. He used his power to draw a blanket over our bodies.

"My mate, I need to mark you now," Fintan said.

I lifted my head. "And I you."

We gazed into each other's eyes, heat, power, and emotion simmering between us. He collected a flower from the nightstand, a small bloom of pale blue and white, that I recalled from our first meeting in the atrium.

He smoothed my hair back with a hand and placed the small flower behind my ear. "The beginnings of your crown." He smiled. "I don't want to fall into the Quiet, but I want to absorb all your memories. I want to find you wherever you are and I hope you feel the same."

"Aye, Fintan," I said. "I want the same."

He sighed. "Good, because I've fallen for my mate."

I kissed his red lips. "I've fallen for my mate, too."

Oh, how I'd fallen for Fintan. His determination to win me over, his kind and gentle nature, his protective streak—he'd wriggled into my heart, and now it belonged to him.

He smiled and pressed a hand to my chest, over my heart. I placed my palm on his chest, over his heart. Our powers flared, the need to mark our mates the most primal force surging inside us.

"Oh," I groaned as his power grew hotter and seared my flesh. My hand wavered on his chest.

Fintan grunted. "Keep going, Niamh, make me yours, be my princess and future queen."

I firmed my palm into the hardness of his chest and let all my power flow between us. Images raced through my head of Fintan's life. His parents, his study in fighting skills, his friends, his lovers. I growled.

"There will be no one but you forevermore," Fintan whispered.

"Aye." My eyes closed under the onslaught of memories. I was ready and willing to accept all of my mate today, and for the rest of eternity, as he accepted my memories at the same time. Accepted all of me, too, apart from one minor detail I needed to tell him many moons from now.

One secret wouldn't be too hard to keep when there was love blossoming between us.

Together we slipped into the Quiet, a world of darkness and memories. A world of learning everything about our mates. When we woke together, we'd share our lives and loves as marked mates, and our future children would be princes and princesses of the Summer Court.

CHAPTER TWELVE
NIAMH

I STRETCHED LAZILY, MY muscles aching like I'd worked all day on the farm reaping barley. Except the room wasn't mine. The bed wasn't mine. A jolt of panic speared through my limbs. I sat up with a start. A soft protest mumbled out of Fintan's lips. Memories flooded back, bringing a smile of joy to my face. This man was mine. I launched myself at him and kissed his cheeks.

Fintan's arms wrapped around my waist, and he held me tight to his firm body.

"Hello, mate," he said with a deep huskiness.

My insides quivered with need. One time with him was not enough and after seeing all his memories, there was much for me to experience with my mate.

"Mate." My lips stretched into a smile against his cheeks.

He stroked a hand down my back.

"How are you after the Quiet? Did my memories hurt you?"

I shifted my lips to his neck. "'Tis all right, Fintan." I suckled his skin. "It was necessary, and I learned a few things." I swiped my tongue across his collarbone.

Fintan groaned. "I hardly think that is fair since you had no memories of lovers."

I raised my head. "Would you prefer I had?"

He lifted his lip and snarled.

I giggled.

"My little vixen."

He rolled us over so he was on top of me.

"You're going to keep me guessing for eternity, aren't you?"

I wriggled my hips against his thick erection. "Not always."

He lowered his lips to mine. The kiss started slow. Soft. Lips against lips. Caressing. Teasing. Then his tongue found mine. He savored me. Drank in my essence as I drank in his. He ran a hand down my side. My skin exploded in sensitive tingles of desire. His fingers splayed across my hip and his thumb brushed across my curls. I kissed him harder. He met my kiss with the same need. For what seemed an eternity, we kissed, his thumb teasing my sensitive mound without ever dipping to my aching entrance.

I ripped my mouth from his. "Fintan, please."

"Please what?" He cocked an eyebrow.

I traced a finger over the swirls of my mating mark on his chest. "I need you inside me."

"I'm learning what my mate likes."

"We have forever."

"Aye."

He hooked his arm under my knee and kissed his way down my stomach.

"But I need to make sure you're ready."

"I'm ready," I huffed.

He swiped his tongue through my damp folds. My back arched off the bed at the sudden soft touch on my eager flesh. He raised my knee and spread me open to his hungry mouth, devouring me with his lips and tongue until the tension in my body grew too much.

"Please," I whispered.

Fintan slid up my body and inside me. I cried out with the completeness of the act. This was so much better than our first time. Our mating marks warmed and sent a pleasant sensation through my veins, adding to the movement of Fintan buried deep. His cock thrust in time to my demanding hips. An obsession overcame me. I needed him hard and fast. I wanted to have him deep inside forever. His lips met mine. I tasted myself on him, heady and erotic.

I mumbled against his lips, "I want to taste you too."

Fintan pumped his hips harder.

I moaned and dug my fingers into his back. He impaled me with his cock in the most pleasurable way. My muscles wound tighter. Clenched him harder. Needed him more. He complied as though he read my mind and I soared high into the clouds of ecstasy. Fintan followed me into the freefall. We drifted down from the ultimate pleasure to settle on the bed tangled in each other's limbs.

"I may have died and flown to heaven."

Fintan rolled off me and scowled. "Don't say that."

"What?"

He rose from the bed. "Dying." He stomped into the bathroom.

I scurried after him. "Fintan?"

He waved his hands, and the enormous tub filled with water. A second wave and flames crackled to life underneath, heating the water almost instantly.

I stepped closer and ran my hands up his back. "I didn't mean it."

He glanced over his shoulder. "I've just found you."

I rubbed his tense shoulders. "We're immortal. We'll have eternity together."

"I'm sorry, my love. Eternity will never be long enough with you. My grandparents thought they had eternity, yet they didn't."

I circled his waist and rested my head on his back. "I'm sorry about your grandparents."

"Me too," he muttered.

"How old were you when they died?" I asked. Even though I'd seen his memories, I sensed a deep need emanating from him to talk about those he'd lost.

"I was rather young. I'd just turned ten years old, but I remember them clearly." He sighed. "They would have loved you."

"Not like your father, then?"

"Father changed when his parents died, he has his own personal issues."

He placed his hands on top of mine.

"He'll come around."

"I don't know, he doesn't seem to like me much."

"He doesn't know you, but when he does, he'll love you, your spirit, and your courage."

He spun, scooped me up into his arms, and stepped into the tub.

"We should wash, see how long we were in the Quiet, and then visit your parents."

He lowered us into the water.

"Oh, my parents. I hope they're not worried." I wriggled out of Fintan's hold.

"Father would have sent word to them." He waved his hand, and the flames settled lower around the tub.

"I love your powers. All I can do is sing." I picked up a bar of soap from beside the tub.

"You did more than sing at the Water Sprite ball—you knocked the Master and me on our asses."

I paused with the soap against my arm. "I did, didn't I?"

"Aye, my amazing mate."

"I never felt the surge of power in my hands before you. It's like you've unlocked my true Fae power."

"You unlocked the power yourself."

"Me?"

"Aye, and perhaps our fated mating had something to do with it. Who knows?"

I washed, contemplating his words. Fintan watched every movement I made, eyes blazing with desire. I handed him the soap and watched him wash. My body grew hotter than the water.

"Is this what it's always like between mates?" I asked.

"What?" He returned the soap and picked up a bottle.

"This all-consuming need to have you touch me, kiss me, be inside me, all the time."

He grinned. "I hope so."

I laughed. The sound echoed in the bathroom, so bright, and airy, and happy. Was that me? I'd never known happiness like this before Fintan.

"Can I wash your hair?"

I bit my lip, nodded, and turned around in the warm water, sending a small amount over the edge to hit the flame with a sizzle. Fintan's powers were soft in their touch. The water ran down my head in a gentle caress. I'd sensed them enough times now to know when he used his powers to touch me. They were a part of him. He massaged his fingers into my scalp. A decadent moan slipped out of my mouth. More water washed the suds away.

"Come." He stood in a rush. "Otherwise we'll never leave my bedroom."

The evidence of his need stood to attention in my face. I licked my lips. Fintan held out his hand. I placed my palm in his and let him pull me to my feet. We stepped out of the bath together. I was happy to see I wasn't the only one battling with my desire. Fintan wrapped me in a towel before drying himself, then strode into the bedroom. I followed him. He wrenched open the doors to his wardrobe and dressed so fast I'd only picked up my dress.

"Surely we can stay a little longer?"

"Being royalty is a drain sometimes." Fintan sighed. "I wish we could stay here together alone for months on end, but royal duty calls. We have my parents to talk to, your parents to inform. They would have sent royal announcements throughout the Summer Court. Then there will be the introductions to the royal aides and guards. There will be an official ball where all the Fae will come and meet you, too. Then, once you're properly introduced here, we'll tour the other castles and kingdoms where you'll be introduced further."

"All that?" I'd never considered the duties of being royalty. I shook the dress. Sparks of luminous blue shone from the threads.

Fintan frowned. "Where did you get that blue gown?"

"Oh, the Water Sprite Master..."

"You can't wear that." He plucked the dress from my hands. "Wait here, I'll fetch you a clean gown."

"Fintan, wait."

But he was already out the door, mumbling about the arrogance of Sir Axis and burning the gown. I smothered a laugh, and walked over to the window, dragged the heavy curtain aside, and stared out at the beauty of the Summer Court. From here on out, this would be my home. With Fintan. As my mate. I touched a hand to my forehead. He had so many memories. I shifted my hand to my chest and his mating mark. The etches of knots and swirls were more than a mark, they were a connection, a tying of two souls. Even now I could sense him, and the distance he'd traveled.

He could always find me, and I him.

The bedroom door snicked open and closed behind me. I turned. Fintan held up a gown in shimmering silver-yellow fabric.

A tiny gasp escaped. "It's beautiful."

"A gown fit for a princess."

I placed a hand to my throat. "Me, a princess?"

"Aye, have you not looked in the mirror?"

I shook my head and raced to the mirror hanging over the set of timber drawers. My face stared back at me the same as always, but upon my head sat a crown of pale blue flowers. The same flower Fintan had produced by the spring, the same flower he'd placed in my hair before marking me. The crown must have formed while we were in the Quiet.

Fintan stepped behind me. "Your crown suits you."

I touched a bloom with a trembling finger. "I never wanted this."

"I know."

Fintan cupped my hand and stroked the flowers with me.

"It's what makes you even more special."

My throat thickened. Tears welled in my eyes. "Fintan, I know this is quick, but I think I may love you."

He smiled so wide, I'd seen no one happier.

"I think I love you too."

I spun around and threw my arms around his neck.

He pecked my lips.
"Get dressed so we can tell your parents."
"Aye," I said.

CHAPTER THIRTEEN
FINTAN

NIAMH WAS RESERVED WHEN we left my bedroom. Our bedroom. I took her quietness as a sign of nerves since Father hadn't welcomed her with open arms like Mother. We found Mother and Father in the rose garden.

"You're awake," Father said.

"How long were we in the Quiet for?" I asked.

"Twas not long. A month."

Niamh's fingers clenched mine harder.

"The gown suits you," Mother said.

She dragged Niamh out of my hand and hugged her.

"And the crown."

Niamh's cheeks flushed pink.

Father folded his arms. "You'll have royal obligations now, Niamh."

Niamh curtsied. "Aye, my King."

Mother tsked. "No more curtsying. You're one of us now. Fae curtsy to you."

"I'll always curtsy to the King," Niamh said.

That produced a smile on my father's face. Every Fae understood the importance of our King.

Mother released Niamh, cupped my face, and tugged it lower to kiss my forehead.

"I'm so happy for you, Fintan. You've chosen well."

"Neither of us had a choice," Fintan said.

"There's always a choice," Mother said. "Some ignore the right ones."

How anyone could ignore choosing their fated mate was beyond me. I scratched my chin. Did Niamh and I have a choice? Had we chosen each other instead of letting fate dictate to us?

Did it matter?

We belonged to each other now.

"Can we discuss royal obligations later? Niamh would like to visit her parents."

Father stiffened a fraction. Mother shot him a hooded look.

"What is it?" I asked, not missing the subtle hints from my parents.

"Are my parents all right?" Niamh asked.

"Aye, your parents are fine," Mother said. "We sent word to them of your mating."

I raised an eyebrow. There was something amiss.

"Let us walk a bit, son."

"Come, Niamh," Mother said. "Let us adjourn to the terrace for tea and refreshments before you travel to Earth."

Niamh glanced at me.

I nodded my head. "I'll join you in a few minutes."

Mother urged Niamh back to the palace. Father and I walked in the other direction.

"But?" I asked when we were out of earshot.

"We've had a rumor reach the Summer Court from Earth," Father said. "Nothing of concern yet."

"What rumor?"

"Humans." He scowled.

"What about them?"

"There was an altercation between a group of humans and a Fae."

"What happened?"

"We don't know. We can't find who the rumor is about." He flicked his robes back and stopped.

"A missing Fae?"

"We can't prove this as we have no way of tracking the Faes and half-bred Faes on Earth. Like I said, rumor."

"But you're concerned?"

"As King of the Fae, of course I'm concerned. The welfare of our people is my priority," he said, his crown of thorns growing agitated with each word he spoke.

"We should command all the Fae to reside here as a precaution."

"We cannot pull people from their lives, son. We'll keep our ears peeled for further news, but until we hear more, there is not much we can do."

He clapped a hand on my shoulder.

"Besides, we've aided humans since the beginning of time. Without us, their Earth would turn into disarray."

"What do I tell my mate?"

"Nothing. There's nothing to tell."

"You want me to lie to my mate?" I flung a surge of power into the air, whipping up a strong breeze.

"'Tis not a lie when there is no truth."

I snorted and let my power drop. "Is that what you tell Mother?"

His eyes narrowed. "What happens between my mate and I is none of your business. You'll speak nothing of this to your mother either."

I shook my head. "Mother will fry your ass if you lie to her."

"That she would." He grinned. "She's aware of the rumor and agrees we need more information."

"But Niamh's family live on Earth."

"And they'll continue to live on Earth like many other Fae."

"She'll worry about them."

"It's an unnecessary worry." He folded his arms.

We glared at each other.

He huffed. "I see what is going through your head, son. You'll tell her as soon as the opportunity arises. We can't have panic amongst our people. That said, I command you not to say anything to Niamh."

I threw up my hands. "You're pulling rank?"

"I am." He nodded. "Niamh's family is comprised of members who can't come through the veil. What do you think would happen if they thought they were in danger and half their family came here?"

I rubbed my forehead. "I don't know."

"No, you were a young lad when the Earth dwelling beings thought they could take down the veil. Many thought they'd be safe from the false Siren Empress in the Summer Court, but they couldn't get in. Father died attempting to talk sense into them."

"Didn't they realize if they took down the veil, there would be no security?"

"People are not always the best at thinking things through before acting." He unfolded his arms. "You need to put your royal duty first."

"I always put my royal duty first." I scowled. "Why do you think I'm not still in my bedroom with my mate?"

He ran an assessing gaze over me and nodded.

"Come," he said. "Your mother and mate are waiting for us. We will join you on your trip to Earth and meet Niamh's parents."

It was as good as saying he believed the rumor. I shoved the thought to the corner of my mind as we walked back to the palace. Niamh sparkled like the brightest jewel—not her dress, but the smile on her face. My heart beat faster. My footsteps grew more urgent to be closer to her.

Father chuckled. "I feel the same way every time I see Orlaith."

"It never fades?"

"No. If anything, it grows stronger."

"Dia." I rubbed a hand over my chest. Niamh's mating mark warmed. "How do you ever do anything except stay in bed?"

He smirked. "Bed is the last place we end up together."

I coughed and choked at the same time.

Father slapped me on the back. "Wait until your mate is in heat."

Niamh stood from her seat. A quizzical smile tipped the corners of her lips. I slid my hands to her waist and kissed her forehead. A Fae woman in heat was irresistible because of the pheromones they emitted. There was no way to predict when it would happen, but they didn't start until a Fae was a hundred years old. Which meant Niamh and I had fifty years before her first heat. Fifty years to practice making a baby. She was irresistible now. When she was in heat... My body stirred at the thought.

I changed the direction of my thoughts. "Ready to see your parents?"

"Fintan, you should eat first," Mother said.

"Mother," I groaned. "I'm two-hundred-years old, and mated. I can decide when I need to eat."

Mother glared at me.

"You should eat," Niamh said.

I sighed. Now I had two women looking after me. I pulled out Niamh's chair, then settled beside her. Mother sipped her tea with a nod. Father sat next to Mother, picked up her hand, and kissed her knuckles. Mother's face softened, and she turned an adoring gaze to him.

A small smile lifted my lips.

I had a small sample of the love I'd build for my mate, and if it grew into anything like the epic love of the Fae King and Queen, then Niamh and I would be the happiest Faes ever.

The King parted the veil to Niamh's family home. We arrived on Earth in a field of golden barley. Ahead stood a moderate-sized white cottage with dark timber shuttered windows and a thatched roof. It was quaint and seemed understated for someone as special as Niamh.

Perhaps her family didn't realize how special she was.

The front door flew open.

Niamh released my hand and ran toward the woman running from the house. They met in a swirl of silver-yellow hair and fabric. Her mother's yellow dress, simple yet beautiful, made Niamh appear the princess she now was in her shiny gown. They swayed side to side, parted, clasped hands, and twirled in the field like they danced to a tune only they could hear.

"Niamh," a man called out while running across the field.

The women parted. Niamh ran to the man. He caught her in his arms and twirled her around by the waist.

Niamh laughed. The purest sound I'd ever heard. Full of sweet happiness. The love for her family was clear on her face and they reflected the love to her. I'd have to convince them to live in the Summer Court with us.

"Niamh." I cleared my throat and sent a surge of power into the wind to ruffle her hair.

She gave me a dreamy smile, tugged her parent's hands, and led them over to us.

"Mother, Father, this is my mate, Prince Fintan."

Her mother curtsied, and her father bowed.

"Please," I said and waved them up. "You're Niamh's parents, there's no need for that."

The King huffed.

"These are my parents, King Diarmuid and Queen Orlaith."

They curtsied and bowed again.

Father looked pleased.

"Your majesty," Niamh's father said. "I'm Eamon O'Keefe and this is my mate Maeve. It's an honor you grace us with your presence on Earth."

"Aye." Father flicked his gaze around the farm. "What does your farm produce?"

"Barley for my famous lager."

"Lager?" The King's eyes sparkled. "I can't remember the last time I drank a good lager."

"Maeve, honey, fetch our guests some refreshments."

"That's unnecessary," I said. "We ate recently."

"Nonsense." Father waved me aside. "Let us get to know our new family in style."

"Niamh, can you give me a hand, please?" Maeve asked. "Eamon, take our guests to the gazebo out the back, 'tis a fine day to sit outside."

Maeve ushered Niamh inside the house and she disappeared from my sight. My stomach churned. Being out of her presence felt like half my heart was missing. I should have offered to help too.

"This way, please," Eamon said. "The women won't be long."

CHAPTER FOURTEEN
NIAMH

"DIA," MOTHER SAID AS she rushed us into the kitchen. "Niamh, I could barely believe the note we received. I wanted to visit the Summer Court to find you, but your father insisted the note was true and we should wait."

"It was." I fetched mugs from the cupboard.

"Stop." She placed her hands on her hips. "Tell me everything. How did this happen? Did your voice trick the Prince? If the King finds out this is all fake, then who knows what he'll do."

"Mother." I left the open cupboard and sat at the kitchen table. "Sit for a minute."

She plonked herself into a chair.

"At first, I thought it was my voice tricking Fintan." I touched a hand to my hair, forgetting I now wore a crown of flowers. My fingers brushed the soft petals of a bloom. "But I felt something for him when I'd felt nothing for another man."

"How can you ever know his feelings are real?" She pressed her fingers to her temples.

"We visited a witch."

"A witch." Mother stood and paced the room. "What did she do?"

"She made a potion to take the call of seduction out of my voice." I longed to tell her the rumors of Siren blood in our family were true, but I'd made a promise to the witch and I wouldn't break it. "It worked, Mother. The potion lets me sing without men falling for me."

She stopped pacing. Her gaze registered the crown on my head, to the gown on my body, but more, the happiness in my smile, the growing love in my eyes.

"No more curse?"

"No, and I won't pass it on to any daughters." I grinned.

Mother let out a long breath. Her shoulders slumped with the exhale. "This is real?"

"Aye, very real. I barely believe it myself."

"Well," Mother rushed into action. "We best put on a good welcome for our new family. The Royals. My daughter is a princess." She squealed.

She fetched Father's famous lager and filled the mugs. "A princess," she muttered over and over.

"I'm still me." I placed the full mugs on a tray. "Your daughter, the one you taught to sing before I could talk."

Mother laughed and lifted the tray. "You used to sing everything, even asking for a piece of bread."

I held the door open for her. "Why wouldn't I? When you sounded so pretty singing. I wanted to be like you."

We walked through the array of flowers in Mother's back garden toward the timber gazebo with vines creeping up the sides and hanging across the top.

"You'll always have a part of me." She sighed. "I suppose you'll live in the Summer Court now?"

"Aye. There are royal obligations I haven't learned of yet."

"I'll miss you." Mother's eyes teared up.

"Now, love, there's no need for tears."

Father took the tray from Mother and placed it on the table.

"This is a merry occasion."

"I knew she wouldn't live with us forever but I thought we'd have longer." Mother sniffed.

"We'd love you to move to the Summer Court," Fintan said.

I snapped my gaze to him and mouthed a silent thank him.

"Oh, we couldn't," Mother said. "Our life is here. The rest of our family."

"They'd be welcome too," Fintan said.

The King stood. "Eamon, Maeve, the Summer Court will always be open to the Fae."

"Ah," Father said and sat back down on the bench seat.

Mother passed a mug to Fintan. He nodded his thanks.

The King reclaimed his seat. "'Tis the way the veil works."

"Once we would have been able to bring our entire families to the Summer Court," Father said. "But now..."

"Eamon's brother is mated to a fox shifter. They have many children and often require our help," Mother said. "A few of their children have married humans, too."

"I understand." The King accepted the mug Mother handed him.

"No," Fintan said. "You should live with us in the Summer Court."

"Fintan," the King said in a warning tone.

Fintan shared a look with the King. They both sipped their lagers.

"Well, they should—for Niamh's happiness," Fintan said.

"Sweet Prince, I can see why you are my daughter's mate." Mother touched Fintan's arm. "We will visit often."

"But..."

"Enough," the King barked.

Father lifted a mug. "Let's toast to the new mates. To Prince Fintan and Niamh."

"To Prince Fintan and Princess Niamh." The King raised his mug.

Mother hurried to pass the Queen a mug. I collected my own and Mother picked up the last one. Everyone raised their drinks and toasted me and Fintan.

"Well." The King grinned. "This is the best lager I've ever tasted."

"Thank you," Father said.

"We'll visit you here too. Family is important," the King said.

The Queen laughed. "You've forgotten the pleasures to be had on Earth."

"I have." The King clasped her hand. "We'll have to visit more often."

Fintan frowned.

I sipped my lager. The tang was like home, always a reminder of my father and the way he tended to the barley, using his power to produce the best lager on Earth. Father launched into a long and animated suggestion of places they should visit if they were planning to visit Ireland more often. The older royals watched my father's wild arm movements and listened attentively, but Fintan stared into the bottom of his mug, a far-off glaze in his eyes.

I leaned into Fintan's side and whispered, "Are you all right?"

He slid his arm around my shoulders. "Aye."

"Are you sure?"

He kissed my forehead. "Let's enjoy this short time with your parents while we're here."

"How long can we stay?"

"The day."

"Is that all?" I pouted.

"Next time we'll organize a longer stay."

"I'd like that." I snuggled into Fintan's side. Not very princess-like, but these were my parents, and they knew me better than anyone but Fintan.

As the sun set across the horizon, I prepared to leave Earth with the Royals. The King swayed a little getting to his feet. The Queen slid an arm around his waist and kept him upright. Upon standing, my father kept his feet, but his ruddy face and glistening eyes gave away his intoxication. Father grinned, wished us well and to visit again soon. Mother's eyes glistened once more as she released me from her hug. I made them promise to come to the Summer Court. And then we were back in the elegant beauty of the palace.

So different, yet so was I.

Fintan led me through the palace to the atrium. The place we'd met. My heart raced, recalling the way I'd felt when I first set eyes on him. Those feelings had grown so much in such a short time.

"It's so peaceful here." My churning emotions settled with the soft trickle of the spring. I walked under the many hanging blooms. The flowers in my crown hummed with power in the atrium when they'd never done so before. It must be the royal connection to the spring.

"There's something you need to know," Fintan said.

"What?" I paused by the pool of water.

He opened his mouth but didn't speak. His intense gaze bored into mine.

"What is it?" I whispered, a sudden churning of unease scampering along my skin.

He shook his head. Blinked slowly, then met my gaze once more. "You know the Spring Baile is the life force of all Fae." He waved his hand and called a ball of water to hover over his hand. "Without this water we'll die."

"I know this place is special."

"Us royal Fae protect the spring. It's why we built the palace around it. We'll always live here. I can't offer you a life outside of being a royal and the obligations that come with the title."

"I don't care where I live or what is required of me so long as I'm with you."

"Our children will live here too. They'll need to protect the spring, as will you."

"I'd protect this special place even if I didn't know how much it meant to every Fae."

Fintan sent the globe of water back to the spring.

I tilted my head. "Will our children have your powers?"

"Aye, they'll be powerful."

I slid my arms around his waist. "Like you."

"You make me weak." He circled my waist with his arms and drew me into the warmth of his body.

"That doesn't sound good." I frowned.

"I'm weak with need for you all the time."

He nibbled my bottom lip.

"Oh." I laughed. "In that case, it sounds perfect because I'm weak with need for you, too. Together we'll be strong."

Fintan brushed a chaste kiss to my lips, and I swayed toward him, eager for more.

"I like your parents," he said.

"Let's not talk about parents right now." I stood on my tiptoes and kissed my mate.

Fintan slipped his tongue past my lips and a soft moan left both our throats.

"Take me to bed," I mumbled against his mouth.

He nibbled my lips. "Bed for the next few times, then I'll show you how we don't need a bed."

"Really?" I raised an eyebrow. "I'm looking forward to everything."

"I'll hold you to that." He squeezed me tighter.

"So long as you hold me to you, I'll be happy."

"As will I, Niamh, as will I."

CHAPTER FIFTEEN
FINTAN

FOUR MONTHS WE'D BEEN traveling to all the kingdoms. To say I'd had enough of parading Niamh around was an understatement. But she'd taken to being a royal with more grace than me. I placed my arm around her shoulders in the wolf shifter's town hall. The different housing and levels of leadership amongst the kingdoms amazed Niamh, and she hadn't even seen them all. What a sheltered life she'd lived on her parent's farm.

They requested she sing at all these events. My hunch was Sir Axis was behind it. I'd find out soon as we were leaving for the Sprite Everglades after Niamh sang. Niamh kissed my cheek, then stood and made her way to the stage.

She glowed with such happiness when she sang now. And she was magnificent at it.

Father shuffled over and sat beside me. "We have found nothing."

At least we'd been able to search for the missing Fae while on this never-ending tour.

"I know. Do you think someone made up the rumor?"

"It's looking more and more likely that was the case." He steepled his hands and rested his chin on them.

"Why though?"

"Someone trying to stir trouble is the most likely scenario."

"What would they get out of it?"

"Unknown." He tapped his finger on his lips. "We'll keep an eye out."

I turned my attention back to Niamh on the stage.

"Your mate has settled into her new role wonderfully."

"She has." My chest expanded.

"Everyone loves her singing."

"Who wouldn't? She sings like the sweetest songbird ever."

Niamh finished her song.

Father lifted his chin from his hands so he could clap. I stood and gave Niamh the resounding applause she deserved. Niamh dipped her head my way and grinned.

"Excuse me, Father." I made my way to the stage, held my arm out for my mate, and helped her down the stairs. "Beautiful, once again, mate."

"Thank you, mate," she said. "Are we heading home now?"

Home. How easily she called the Summer Court home.

"For a quick stop to change clothes then we're heading to the Sprite Everglades."

Her arm stiffened in my hold.

"Relax. It will be fine. I'll be by your side."

"That's what I'm worried about. You got in a sword fight because of me last time we were there."

I chuckled. "I'd get in a sword fight for you anytime I needed to."

"That's not setting my mind at ease."

"How about this? I promise not to get in a sword fight tonight."

She relaxed and squeezed my arm as we walked over to our designated table. Mother and Father stood.

Trick, the wolf shifter alpha, rushed forward and bobbed his head. "Thank you for gracing us with your presence, your highnesses. It was a true honor meeting your new princess and hearing her sing. May you live long and prosperous lives."

"Our pleasure, Trick," Father said.

"Diarmuid." Trick shook hands with the King. "It would be nice to see you more often on Earth."

"I will keep your request in mind." His lips formed into a tight line.

Trick dipped his head, then turned to the crowded hall. "Everyone, please thank the Fae Royals for their visit. I'm afraid their time with us is up."

The wolf shifters howled.

Father parted the veil in a dazzling display of rainbow colors and we returned to the Summer Court.

"That was enjoyable," Mother said. "Freshen up, then we leave again soon."

"Aye, Mother."

Niamh and I hurried back to our bedroom. With each step, I slid open a button on my shirt until it hung open.

She giggled. "Do we have time?"

I flung open our bedroom door with my powers, urged her into the room and stripped off the rest of my clothes.

"We always have time." I ripped her dress from her body with my powers.

"Fintan," she gasped.

"What? The royal seamstress will make another." I scooped her up into my arms and strode for the bed. We'd yet to venture far from the comfort of the mattress, but I didn't care where I had her, so long as I did.

I crawled down her body.

"We don't have time for this," she said, spreading her legs, as eager for me as I was for her.

"Sir Axis can wait." I set to devouring my luscious mate.

"Prince Fintan, Princess Niamh." Axis dipped his head, a wicked smile stretching his lips. "A pleasure to see you again."

"Thank you for inviting us," Niamh said, always so polite.

"Your majesty, your highness." Axis bowed to my parents.

"Sir Axis, we appreciate your warm welcome," Father said.

"Always an honor for the Fae to visit. It's a shame we can't visit you." His smirk dropped.

"Aye, it is," Father said. "But you know as well as I do 'tis nothing I can do to change that."

"Yes, well." He nodded at the ballroom. "Please join the rest of my people, and I promise this ball won't end in anyone being added to a harem." He winked.

I clenched my fists.

The King and Queen wandered into the ballroom.

"Axis," I snapped. "What are you playing at?"

"Nothing, young prince." He tipped his nose up and inhaled. "I smell you've truly mated now."

Niamh wrinkled her nose.

I tugged her into my side. "That's not your business."

"Oh, it is. You see, that song she sang at my last ball was unique." He ran a hand down his shirt. At least he wore one this time. "Tell me, do you still sing the same, Niamh?"

Niamh squared her shoulders and looked down her nose at Axis. "I sing even better."

He threw his head back and laughed. "Sweet songbird, you have fire in you too. I like it. Please join the party and I'd love to hear you sing again tonight."

I nodded at the ballroom. "Go on ahead, Niamh, I'd like a further word with Axis."

Niamh scooted out of my arms and made her way over to where my parents sat at a table overflowing with an abundance of blue flowers, sparkling golden candles, and mountains of refreshments. If I could say anything about the Water Sprites, it was they knew how to party in style.

"What is this word you'd like, Fintan?"

I spun to face Axis. "Do not disrespect Niamh ever again."

He held up his hands. "I meant no disrespect. But if I remember rightly, you were the one who disrespected me in my kingdom no less."

"She's my fated mate. What did you expect me to do?"

"Hmm, a fated mate." He glanced at Niamh. "I can't argue with fate now, can I?"

"No, you can't." I crossed my arms.

Axis slapped me on the shoulder. "Perhaps instead of this hostility, we can work together?"

"On what?"

"I understand you have a missing Fae."

I narrowed my eyes. "How do you know that?"

"We are excellent spies, young prince. You'll do well to remember that."

"What do you want from me in return?"

"I want Niamh to sing at all my balls."

"Done," I said without hesitation. Niamh would be happy to sing, anyway.

"That easy? I expected more fight from you like last time."

I chuckled. "I fought for what was mine last time, and I'd fight for her again if I needed to. Since you seem to be charmed by my mate, I suspect you won't let any harm come to her."

"She is a stunning specimen."

"Besides, I'll be by her side to make sure of that too."

"Did you just invite yourself to my balls?"

"I did." I cocked an eyebrow. "And I'm looking forward to each and every one of them."

Blue sparks flickered under his skin. My power responded and swirled to my hands. Axis's lips spread into a toothy grin.

"We could flop them out and compare sizes," he said.

I rolled my eyes. "Doesn't matter whose is bigger, Niamh will only ever have mine from the first time to the last."

"Damn, she was a virgin. I should have fought you harder."

My power whipped around his hair.

Axis chuckled. "This is going to be such fun seeing you two so often."

He strode into the ballroom, leaving me to glare at his back. Cocky bastard, but if what he said was true, and they were excellent spies, then I needed him. I wasn't sure how he needed Niamh to sing for him, but I'd be by her side to find out.

Speaking of Niamh's side, I made my way over to my mate, but Axis beat me there.

"Princess Niamh, it would be a great honor if you'd sing for us tonight." Axis bent at the waist. "Your mate has accepted my invitation for you to sing at our future balls, too. I hope that is okay with you."

Niamh tilted her head and gave him a demure smile. "Of course, singing at your balls is satisfactory with me.

My mate knows this." She stood. "I'd love to sing tonight too."

I offered her my arm. She hooked her arm through mine and together we stepped toward the stage.

"What's going on?" she whispered.

"Politics." I kissed her cheek. "We need to keep the Water Sprites on our good side."

"Very well," she said. "One song coming up to keep them on our side."

She made her way to the center of the stage. A bright spotlight flared on her. Niamh's gown shone an elegant midnight blue with delicate white stitching on the bodice. Every gown she wore, I thought her more and more beautiful. It wasn't the gowns, though. It was the way she grew in strength after every royal engagement. The way she sang so freely now. And the way she gazed at me with such love in her eyes.

"Thank you all for your lovely welcome," Niamh said. "Sir Axis has requested a song."

A round of applause exploded in the room. The other Water Sprites were as eager as Axis to hear her sing again. I set my shoulders back and tamped my power down even though no man would wrongly believe she was their mate. The last time we were here sat heavy in my mind.

One life,
Two lives,
A bounty of lives.
We all live,

We all breathe,
We all have a heartbeat.
Yesterday we were acquaintances,
Today we are friends,
Tomorrow we are comrades.
Our lives are different,
But the same.
Our powers are pure,
Natural, Us.
We will always be,
We will always stay,
Us.
What say you?
Clasp my hand,
And we'll dance
All night
Rejoicing in our new
Relationship.

I clapped along with the rest of the Water Sprites. Niamh dipped her head and stepped from the stage.

"You're impressive," I murmured.

She lifted her love-filled eyes to mine.

"Well," Axis said, stepping in front of us. "That was unexpected."

"What did you expect?" Niamh asked.

"I expected," he drawled, "a certain reaction from my people, yet your voice seems to be missing that note this time. Why?"

"I don't know what you're talking about," Niamh said.

"Come now, little songbird, we both know what I'm talking about. Spill."

Niamh's jaw tightened.

"She drank a potion to relieve her of that particular note," I said.

"What was in the potion?"

I dropped my gaze to Niamh.

She shrugged. "I'm not sure. The witch's cauldron was already bubbling when I got there."

He smoothed his hands down his pants. "Does the witch in question have a name?"

"Saltine," I said.

"Oh, she's good, I'll give her that." He shoved his hands in his pockets. "I liked your song, Niamh. Please enjoy the rest of the night. Eat, drink, dance."

"Thank you," Niamh said, then turned to me. "Fintan let us dance."

"Aye, my mate." I spun her onto the dance floor and brought our bodies together. "Shall we dance like the Water Sprites?"

She wrapped her arms around my waist and laid her head on my chest. Wrapped in each other's arms, we danced around the floor while the musicians played their melody. The music was soft and dreamy. Niamh snuggled closer.

"You handled Axis well. In fact, you've handled everyone well. You were born to be a princess."

She tipped her chin up. "Your memories have helped me learn how to act."

"Perhaps, but I think it's all you, and how special you are."

"How special we are," Niamh said.

"We," I said and smiled. "My mate and I, together, forever."

"Forever," she whispered.

I lowered my head and claimed her lips with a kiss, and it wasn't the need to show every Water Sprite in this room Niamh was mine and I was hers. It was the need to be with her in any way I could, and right now, this was how we could be together. Soon these endless parties would end and we'd settled down in the palace to a more sedate lifestyle. Not that being a royal would be quiet, but it would be more normal than this.

Niamh's lips vibrated with a quiet moan. I ended the kiss with great reluctance we weren't alone and in our bedroom. Soon we'd venture out of the bedroom too. Maybe next time we were at the Sprite ball we'd find somewhere to venture, too. A smile tugged my lips into a broad grin.

"Why are you smiling?" she asked.

"Because I have you."

PART TWO

A NEW PRINCE

CHAPTER SIXTEEN
FINTAN
1450

I T HARDLY SEEMED LIKE fifty years had passed with my exquisite mate. We sat on the shore of the lake watching the sunrise like we did every morning. Niamh had wedged herself between my legs and rested her head on my chest. I'd wrapped my arms around her shoulders and listened to her quiet breaths as the sun shifted over the horizon in a stunning display of pinks and purples.

"Are you looking forward to your ball tonight?" I inhaled her sweet aroma. My brow tightened. Her scent possessed an even sweeter tang than usual.

"Aye. My mother is looking forward to singing at the ball."

She rested her chin on my arms.

"'Tis not every day you turn one hundred."

"Still think of me as a young?"

She tilted her head to the side to smile at me, full of teasing humor.

I chuckled. "It was a slip of the tongue. I have never for one second thought of you as too young. Dia, mate, what do you take me for?"

She laughed.

I brushed a kiss across her laughing lips. She stopped laughing to kiss me back. Our kiss deepened. She always kissed me like I was her everything.

Niamh ended our kiss on a gasp and lunged to her feet, clutching her stomach.

"Niamh, what's wrong?" I stood and reached for her.

She swatted my hand. "I feel strange."

"In what way?" I dropped my hands to my side.

A delicate pink tinged her cheeks. "I enjoy kissing you, but this time was different. It felt like I should kiss you until our mouths bled." She breathed faster. "I need you, Fintan, more than I ever have."

"It's all right, my love."

"It's not." She paced to the edge of the water in her indigo-colored gown.

Her delicious scent ripened. Every muscle in my body tightened with a need for my mate. Which was normal, but rational thought fled my body, which wasn't normal. I sucked in a breath through my teeth. I tasted her. Her need. Her heat.

"Niamh, you're in heat." I clenched my fingers.

"Heat?" She spun in a twirl of indigo, matching the sky.

"Aye." I stalked her like a beast about to pounce. "Your scent," I growled.

Niamh's eyes widened. "Fintan, wait. The castle is full of guests for my birthday party. We can't lock ourselves in your bedroom and ride out my heat." She backed up a step, but her nipples hardened and poked the front of her dress.

"You're right." I stalked closer. "We won't go anywhere."

"What? Here?" She clutched the fabric of her dress and lifted it above her ankles.

"Oh, aye, mate. Here. Right now. We've already ventured outside the bedroom, anyway." I unbuttoned my shirt.

Niamh's gaze heated. "I... Oh, I can't think." She touched her temple.

"No, you need me and I need you." I stripped my pants.

She dropped her gaze to my erection and moaned. "Fintan."

I stepped closer. Her chest heaved inside her dress. Soon I'd have her out of it.

"You can't fight this. It's pure nature to feel this way." She scanned the shore. "What if someone comes?"

"Oh, you'll be coming multiple times."

She snorted. "That's not what I meant, and you know it. My parents are here. And the castle is full."

I'd got within grabbing distance while she babbled and swooped her into my arms. She clung to me like she'd wanted me to touch her all along, and she had. I devoured her lips. Her lush scent grew stronger, if that was possible. I needed to lick her. Bury myself inside her.

I threw her over my shoulder.

She shrieked.

"Hush or they will come and see what the noise is."

She snapped her mouth shut.

I waved my hand and called lily pads across the water to our feet. One by one, the large green disc-shaped leaves overlapped each other until there was enough for a floating bed. I lowered Niamh onto the mattress of water lilies.

She smiled and stroked the pads with her hands. "You always surprise me with your powers."

I kneeled on the pads and sent a gust of wind, blowing us from the shore of the lake to the middle. Niamh parted her legs. I dragged her dress up her body and over her head, rolled it into a ball, and placed the fabric under her head.

"Niamh." I traced a finger from her collarbone to her hipbone. "I'm a little insane with need for you right now."

"I'm insane with need for you." She cupped her breasts. "My nipples ache."

I lowered my head and suckled one nipple, then the other. "What else aches?"

"Lower." Her eyes twinkled with lust.

I kissed her stomach. "Here?"

She shook her head. "Lower."

"My little vixen, tell me what you need."

"You, all of you."

I swiped my tongue through her folds. "Like that?"

She tugged my hair.

"Fintan, now is not the time for playing."

She met my smirk with a frustrated huff. I speared my tongue into her opening, tasting the sweetness of her heat. She tasted so good I could lap at her juices for the entire day. Since she was only in heat for one day, I intended to do just that out here, floating in the sunshine on the lake. Her slickness coated my lips and chin. I pressed into her harder, deeper. Her legs quivered, a sure sign she was close to shattering. The best sensation ever.

I tugged her hips closer to me. Buried my face in the intoxicating aroma of her desire. Breathed her in. My cock hardened and throbbed with the need to be coated by her slickness. A growl rumbled from my lips. Niamh exploded with the vibrations. Her body jerked and shook as wave after wave of release pulsed against my tongue and lips. I stroked her spasming muscles. Her cries of delight were the best songs she had ever sung to me.

"Fintan," she rasped.

I dragged my tongue to her hard clit and thrust two fingers into her.

"Fintan," she cried, her back arching off the lily pads.

I pumped my fingers, lost to the sensation.

"Enough," she growled and shoved my shoulders.

The lily pads rippled in the water. I sent my power to settle them. My thoughts were clearer now I wasn't feasting on her eager flesh.

Her gaze roamed my body. "I need more."

"Take what you need from me." I stroked my cock.

She swiped her tongue across her teeth, crawled across the small distance and onto my lap.

"Shite," I mumbled as she lowered herself onto my cock. It was all I could do to keep still and let her take what she needed from me like I'd promised.

Niamh slid up and down my cock. Her knees rose, her hips slammed down. Fast. I cupped her buttocks. Her skin was so soft. My balls pulled up tight. Heat licked its way down my spine and settled in the place we were joined. If she didn't come again soon, I'd beat her to it and that wasn't what either of us wanted. I urged her closer to me. Her pelvis ground down the front of mine.

There. That was the spot.

Her body tightened. Niamh's warm breath brushed against my neck. Her lips followed, then her tongue. I urged her to ride me faster. Her breasts brushed against my chest. The hard peaks of her nipples begged for my attention. I'd give them hours of attention before her heat was over.

I couldn't take the intensity of her slickness a moment longer. Niamh dug her fingers into my shoulders. One more slam down and she came. Merciful goodness. I thrust up into her undulating body and let my orgasm claim me. Claim her. Mark her. Fill her with what her body demanded while in heat.

What she needed to make a baby.

I kissed her forehead and smiled.

Niamh gave me a dreamy smile in return.

"Better?" I asked.

"Aye." She placed a palm on her mating mark on my chest. "I didn't think I'd come into heat the day I turned one hundred."

I kneaded her buttocks with my fingers. "I'm not complaining."

"Me either," she said. "A little baby Fintan will be adorable."

"Or a little baby Niamh."

"Either." She squinted across the lake to the shore. "Someone is coming."

"It's Grieg." I'd recognize him anywhere, even from this distance. Grieg had been by my father's side since before I was born.

Niamh wriggled off my lap and clutched her dress to her chest.

I laughed. "He can't see you. We're too far out."

Grieg stopped where I'd left my clothes. He lifted a hand and waved. I used my power to send a breeze from behind us to Grieg. His already stiff stance stiffened further, then he spun on his feet on the sandy shore and marched back the way he'd come.

"You didn't even tell him anything," Niamh said.

"I didn't need to. Your heat scent told him everything he needed to know. He'll return to the palace and inform the King. No one else will bother us."

"So, we're staying out here until my heat is over?" She raised her eyebrows.

"It's only one day." I shrugged. "We could go back to the palace and have every man clamoring for you."

Niamh shuddered. "No, thank you. I've been there. I have no wish to return."

"Then come here, I can scent your need is growing."

"You can scent my heat?"

"Aye, and it's the most delectable aroma ever."

"You like the way I smell?" She dropped the dress.

"I love your aroma every day, but today..."

Her body slammed into mine and we tumbled back on the lily pads with a splash. I had the presence of mind to stabilize our floating bed with my powers before I let my mate take what she needed from me all over again.

After that, I'd give her more. And more. Until her heat was over, and she carried our child.

A new Fae royal.

CHAPTER SEVENTEEN
NIAMH

F IFTY YEARS AS FINTAN'S mate. As a princess. As a protector of the spring. I never failed to be filled with awe whenever I walked into the atrium surrounding the spring, but today I was in awe for another reason, too.

Today we'd meet our baby.

"Fintan," I puffed out between clenched teeth. "I need my mother."

"Father sent someone to fetch her." Fintan paced the atrium. "She'll be here."

I rubbed my very pregnant stomach. The contractions were coming hard and fast now.

My face flushed at the reminder of how we'd made our baby.

Fintan was a creative lover. I loved anything and everything he did to me. But I did not like what this baby was doing while trying to leave my body.

"Is it meant to hurt this much?" I panted.

"Aye." Queen Orlaith rubbed my back. "This is normal."

I narrowed my eyes. "Like my body is trying to rip me in half?"

Fintan paused his pacing to kneel at my feet. "I'm sorry, my love."

I stroked a hand through the length of his hair. "It'll be worth it."

"Every Fae birth is worth the price of the pain," the Queen said. "But a royal birth is extra special."

A contraction clenched my stomach. I tugged Fintan's hair in my fist. He gritted his teeth but took it.

"Argh," I wailed. "The baby is coming now."

The Queen circled her arms around my chest from behind. "Lean on me if you need to."

"You want me to—" I pushed down with the contraction.

Fintan eased my dress up to my waist.

I puffed out a breath. "Give birth standing up?"

"Gravity will work for you," the Queen said. "Fintan will catch the baby."

I laughed, then groaned as another contraction took hold. With my stomach clenching, I pushed down, my focus on the place the most pain throbbed.

"I see a head," Fintan said. "Spread your legs a little more."

I bit my lip.

Fintan chuckled. "That's how we got here."

"Fintan," I gasped. "Your mother."

"I'm sure she knows how heat and mating works." He winked.

Another contraction wracked my body. I tugged his hair and went with the urge to push. A shriek ripped from my lungs. Everything faded to the pain and insistent urge to force the baby out of my body. Fintan and the Queen talked to me, but the intense pounding of my blood made them sound like they were under water. One ear-piercing scream and an almighty push, and the pain stopped.

Fintan stared at the blood-covered bundle in his arms.

"Fintan?" I whispered.

"It's a boy," he whispered in awe.

"Quick," the Queen said, "send your powers into the baby."

"What?" I stuttered.

"Now," she urged.

Fintan's palms glowed as he held the baby. I touched my hands to our precious little boy's feet and sang, sending my power into his warm, sticky body.

Fifty years ago a prince courted me,
My mate found me.
He gave me this life,
He gave me you.
Nine months ago a prince wooed me,
My mate loved me.
He gave me his seed,
He gave me you.
Today a prince encouraged me,

My mate loved me.
He gave me his strength,
He gave me our son.

With every word, my power grew until both our powers glowed and lifted our baby from our hands into the air. Our son, the newest royal, a prince, cried. I sucked in a relieved breath. The Queen eased me to the ground. The baby floated back into Fintan's arms. He placed our baby in my embrace. A dainty creature with pale silver down on his head, rosy cheeks, mouth pursed as though in contemplation. The baby opened his eyes, light blue and indigo-rimmed. Even at this age, he was the epitome of Fae royalty.

"Hello, son." I stroked a finger down the side of his face. Somewhere in the striking beauty of this new royal was a piece of me.

Fintan draped an arm around my shoulders and placed a hand on our baby. "Welcome, little prince."

"He's perfect," the Queen said.

"He is," I said. I'd seen nothing more perfect than our son. Maybe one day I'd have the chance to think the same about a daughter.

"What is his name?" she asked.

"Rian," Fintan said. "Little Prince."

"He won't be little forever." I stroked the soft skin on his face again.

"No, he won't," Queen Orlaith said. "Fintan was that tiny once. Now look at him, a father. I'm so happy. The future of the Fae Royals is right here."

A tiny rumble of thunder cracked over the palace. At least it wasn't inside the palace as what happened when the Queen was angry.

"Perhaps you should tell Father he has a grandson," Fintan suggested.

"Of course. He'll be happy too."

The Queen rushed from the atrium. Fintan let out a sigh and shuffled me and our baby closer to him.

"My mother didn't make it to the Summer Court in time." I sniffed.

"I'm sorry we didn't have time to fetch her. If they lived here, this wouldn't have happened." His lips firmed.

"You've asked them for the last fifty years. I doubt they'll change their minds." I didn't understand why every time we visited my parents on Earth, Fintan tried to get them to come live in the Summer Court. I loved my parents, but visiting Earth wasn't hard for Fae. A swipe of a hand and we could part the veil and step through to our destination with ease. It was easier than traveling on Earth.

"Even now they have a grandson?"

"Not likely." The rumors in my mother's family kept them away from the Summer Court. Father's family were such a mixed bag of marriages, he wouldn't leave them alone since he was the most respected member of their family. I stroked a finger over Rian's forehead. "I need to wash up and Rian, he also needs clothing and feeding."

Fintan scooped me and our baby up into his arms with ease. "Let's head back to our wing and you can clean up while I dress the Little Prince."

My heart swelled. "You're smitten with him."

"Aye." Fintan grinned.

"Me too."

A few hours later, we'd bathed, dressed, and fed baby Rian. He was ready to meet his grandparents. Fintan carried our baby in one arm and kept me in the embrace of his other as we walked through the palace.

Grieg swept down the marble hallway. "The King and Queen request your presence in the great chamber."

Fintan nodded.

Grieg disappeared around a corner. I'd lived here for fifty years and the many halls still confused me. Fintan urged me to continue along our path. A quiver of nerves fluttered in my stomach. The King still intimidated me to this day. The way his crown swirled around his head whenever he looked at me made me wonder if he knew I wasn't a full-blooded Fae, and that I had Siren blood in my family tree. I flicked my gaze to our sleeping baby in Fintan's arms. Rian was the image of Fintan, silver hair, soft red lips, and dark eyebrows.

What would Fintan say when he found out about the Siren blood in my family?

My foot caught in the hem of my dress. I stumbled a step.

"Are you all right?"

Fintan tightened his arm around my waist.

I nodded.

His brow puckered in concern. "If you're too tired, we can go back to bed. My parents can wait."

"No." I thrust a hand to his arm. "They should meet him now. Can we see my parents afterward?"

His frown turned into a scowl. "I don't think that's wise."

"Why not?" I lifted my hand. "They should meet their grandson too."

"But you're tired and we'd have to travel to Earth, and..." His lips firmed.

"Fintan, we heal quickly. I'm already healed from giving birth, especially since you filled the bathtub with the spring's water."

We paused at the door to the great chamber.

Fintan kept his gaze on our baby. He clenched the handle and shoved the door open with no explanation.

Queen Orlaith rushed over to us and gathered the baby into her arms. "Oh, my, he's so precious. I forgot how little babies were. It was so long ago we had Fintan."

King Diarmuid rose from his chair and kissed her cheek. "Two hundred and fifty years ago. I'd hoped we'd have more children."

"As did I," she said, her eyes welling with tears.

"Don't cry." The King circled her waist and drew her into his body. "Fae heats are unpredictable. That's why we value every birth. Babies are our greatest treasure."

A surge of tears sprung to my eyes. I sniffed to hold them back.

The King peered into my face. "Thank you for this great privilege, Niamh. A new prince." He lifted the baby out of the Queen's arms and held him high in the air. "Rian, you shall one day be King too."

A sob burst from my mouth, and the tears fell.

Fintan gathered me in his arms. I cried. I couldn't stop the tears. If Rian would be king one day, that would mean King Diarmuid would be dead, and Fintan. I sobbed louder. Fintan would be dead, too.

"Great going, Father." Fintan rubbed my back.

"What did I say?"

"How do I know?" Fintan asked.

I kept crying.

"Hush, Niamh."

The Queen stroked my hair. "'Tis the baby hormones making you this way."

I sniffed. Fintan shoved a hankie into my hand. I scrubbed my face and battled the tears until they subsided.

"Sorry," I rasped. "I believe you are right, Queen Orlaith. I miss my parents, too. Can we go see them now?"

"Of course, my dear," the King said and eased the baby into my arms. "We'll see you when you get back. I sent word to them, so I'm not sure why they didn't arrive in time for the birth."

"Father," Fintan said.

"Your mate wants to visit with her parents." The King stroked the baby's head. "There's no reason the new prince shouldn't visit their farm."

Fintan frowned, but said, "Very well." He waved his hand and parted the veil in a shimmering display of his power.

I stepped up to the veil. Fintan placed a hand on my elbow and guided us through the shimmering haze. We exited in front of my parents' house. Gray smoke billowed from the chimney into the muted blue-gray sky filled with thick clouds. A chilly breeze blew across the barley. Good thing Fae didn't feel the cold.

Fintan hustled us to the door and knocked. "We shouldn't have come."

"The weather is a bit bleak."

Father opened the door. His eyes widened and his mouth dropped open. "You had the baby."

"Aye," Fintan said. "We sent word Niamh was in labor."

"Come in." He flung the door wide. "We didn't receive word."

Fintan flicked a look over his shoulder and urged me into the house.

"Maeve," Father bellowed.

"What's all the ruckus?" Mother walked out of the kitchen, wiping her hands on an apron. "Niamh?" She dropped the flour-covered apron and rushed over. "You had the baby. Why didn't you tell me?"

Fintan and Father exchanged a glance. What was up? Fintan said he sent word to my parents. Did he or didn't he? Why didn't my parents know?

Rian opened his mouth and let out an almighty cry.

"Oh." Mother scooped him out of my arms into hers. She placed the baby on her shoulder and patted his back. "We upset the wee tot with all our noise. Shh...?"

"Rian. A boy." Fintan grinned. "A prince."

"Shh, Rian." Mother patted his back and paced the sitting room.

"He has a bit to say," Father said.

"Aye." Fintan settled into a chair.

I sat next to him and let Mother have time with her grandson. She wouldn't get to see him much, living on Earth. I sighed. Now I understood why Fintan asked them so often to move to the Summer Court.

"I wish you'd come live in the Summer Court," I said.

Mother stopped pacing. "Our home is here on Earth."

"But the baby?"

"Niamh is right," Fintan said. "You should come live in the Summer Court."

"Prince Fintan, we've discussed this many times and our answer will always be no," Father said.

Fintan patted my hand and stood. "The King is looking forward to your next brew of lager. I'd love to look at your crops."

"They're looking good, as always." Father stood taller. "Come have a look."

"I'll be just outside," Fintan said. "Stay here. It's much too windy for the baby."

I raised an eyebrow.

Father opened the front door for Fintan and they disappeared outside.

"What was that about?" I waved a hand at the door.

Mother shrugged. "Secret lager business."

I laughed. Rian whimpered. Mother sang a lullaby. I closed my eyes. The words were familiar, and the sleepy lure from the power in her voice. She'd sung the songs to me when I was younger, and now she sang them to my son. It was fitting being here, sharing this moment with my mother. I was tired, full of new intense emotions for my baby, but I wouldn't have it any other way.

CHAPTER EIGHTEEN
FINTAN

E AMON RAN HIS HAND across the tops of the barley. "This is a good yield."

"Mmm hmm." I scanned the horizon looking for movement, or a sign my father's messenger had come here.

"You didn't want to look at the barley, did you?"

"No. I wanted to look for the messenger."

Eamon cupped his hand over his eyes. "No one has been here for days. Are you sure a messenger came here?"

"Aye, Father and I were in the library when Grieg informed us Niamh was in labor. I heard him send the order."

The wind dropped to absolute stillness.

"Do you have a Fae with power over the wind nearby?"

"On the other side of the forest is my cousin Nessa, who moved in recently and she has the power over the wind. She doesn't normally send the wind to howl as much as it has today, but she's stopped now."

I swung in the forest's direction. "How far?"

"A good ten-minute walk."

"Is she your closest neighbor?"

"Aye."

"I'll visit her. Stay here. I'll be back soon."

"Why?" He dropped his hand from his forehead.

I sighed.

"Are you concerned about the welfare of the messenger?"

"Aye."

Eamon scanned the barley field. "What aren't you telling me?"

My fingers stopped tapping. "A few Earth living Fae may have gone missing, but there is no way for us to know for certain in the Summer Court even if they actually existed." I scanned the barley field again. "I wish you'd come and live in the Summer Court."

"You keep asking me that, and I keep telling you, we won't leave our family."

"But Niamh is your only daughter." My fingers tapped faster.

"She is, and we love her, but the Summer Court is not a permanent home for us. I wouldn't be able to make my famous lager there. Besides, we have an extensive family here on Earth. A family who wouldn't be able to visit us there and they all look to me for guidance."

"But you could visit them here." I unfolded my arms.

"'Tis not the same and you know it. The King would never rule the Summer Court from a different world," Eamon said.

He was right, and it settled like a ball of dirt inside my stomach.

Eamon frowned. "If the messenger is missing, and others have gone missing, we could be next."

"There's no need to panic." I placed a calming hand on his shoulder. "Your farm is remote and the ones we can't find originated from Germany. Please keep this information to yourself. The King would have my hide if he found out I'd shared this with you."

"What is the King doing about it?"

"We are searching, but we've found no clues." I removed my hand. "I'll check on your cousin."

"I'll wait outside until you return, then the women won't be able to question me about your absence."

"Niamh seems very emotional since she gave birth."

He managed a small smile. "Maeve was the same after Niamh was born. She was a hot mess, doted on our little baby, and sung all the time. It's no wonder Niamh is such a talented singer."

"She's phenomenal. Fae fill the Summer Court ballroom when she sings. You should visit more often."

"We will, even more with the baby, and this..." He threw his hands up in the air like he didn't know what to do with them.

"I won't be long." I walked toward the forest.

Eamon was smart. I wished he and his mate would move to the Summer Court for good. I skirted the sizable barley field, stepped under the trees into the forest, and onto the small path leading the way through the greenery. My feet slipped on the moss-covered ground, and power swirled to my hands, reacting to the eerie quietness lurking amongst the twisted tree trunks. All my senses went on high alert as I continued through the forest and out the other side. A small log cabin backed up to the forest, the intoxicating scent of a Fae in heat wafting from within. I clenched my fists and pounded on the door. Even mated, the aroma tested my restraint.

"Who's there?" A feminine voice squeaked.

"Prince Fintan."

"Shite," a male voice grunted.

A flurry of movement creaked the floorboards inside the cabin and the front door flew open. A slight woman stood wrapped in a sheet, her reddish-blonde hair a mass of messy curls and a pink hue tinging her skin. Behind her was one of the royal attendants, yanking on his red pants.

"I see you didn't deliver your message." I scowled.

"Prince Fintan, I'm so sorry." He wrenched on his shirt and shuffled in front of the woman to kneel at my feet. "Please forgive me."

My power exploded into a slithering coil of smoke ropes and shackled the man.

The woman sobbed. "Please don't hurt him."

I tightened the ropes and reached for the veil, intent on sending the man back to the Summer Court.

"Please." She dove to her knees and wrapped her arms around his neck. "Your majesty, it's not his fault. I intersected him when he arrived. He would have delivered the message if it wasn't for me."

I flicked a glance from his bowed head to the woman. Her heat scent grew stronger. Dia, it was no wonder the man got sidetracked. I remembered Niamh's heat nine months ago when we'd spent the day floating on lily pads pleasuring each other.

"Next time deliver the message first."

"Thank you." He raised his head.

I released the smoke ropes. "Finish this, then head back to the Summer Court. The King will have something further to say in this matter though."

He gulped, but ran a heated look over the woman. A man couldn't help the draw of a Fae in heat, and if the woman had asked him to copulate with her, he wouldn't have been able to say no. Father would understand that too, but he'd punish the man with time in prison.

I headed back to the forest. The door clicked shut behind me. The woman squealed in delight. I paced quicker, needing to get back to my mate, my love, the mother of my child, my everything.

The eerie sensation returned the moment I ducked under the trees. The moss appeared to move as though alive. Tricks of my eyes or magic?

"Who's there?" I asked.

A voice cackled. "Just me."

A familiar voice. My tense muscles eased a fraction.

"Saltine, what brings you to these woods?"

The witch glided from behind a tree and tipped back the hood of her black cloak. "To see you, of course."

"How did you know I'd be here?"

"I know a lot of things, young king." She circled me.

I shook my head. "I'm not the king."

"Not yet." She stopped in front of me and tilted her head. "It is inevitable."

"Perhaps." I frowned.

"Congratulations on the birth of your son."

"How did you know he'd been born?"

She lifted the hood back onto her head. "It was inevitable, too. What's coming is also, there is no stopping it."

"What's coming?"

"Many things." She lifted a hand with a brown vial. The liquid inside swirled like smoke.

"So much pain and suffering." She twirled the vial in her hand. "But this way there will at least be enough for us to continue—any other way and we'd all disappear." She dropped the vial.

A cloud of brown smoke filled the air between us. I coughed and waved my hands in front of my face. By the time the smoke cleared, Saltine had disappeared.

Strange witch.

Even stranger, her finding me here. What was with her? And her words? The hairs on the back of my neck rose. A sense of dread filled me. Pain and suffering. I didn't need that today when I should be happy with a new son and a mate who loved me like I was the most important being in her life.

She was mine. And now our son joined her.

I'd love them both forever.

I returned to her parents' farm. Eamon paced in front of the house, his hands glowing golden. He spotted me and stopped.

"No need to worry. Your sister is in heat and sidetracked the messenger," I said.

"Ah." Eamon's stance relaxed. "Poor sod. He had little choice then."

I chuckled and opened the door. The sight of Niamh asleep on their couch caused all thought of the witch's words to vanish. This, here, was what mattered. This moment when I'd get to cherish my mate and the joy she'd brought into my life.

"You should stay the night," Maeve whispered, still cuddling our son.

I kneeled beside Niamh and brushed my knuckles across her cheek. She blinked her eyes open. Beautiful eyes the color of crushed moonstone. I'd spent many hours gazing into her eyes, and I could spend many more.

"Fintan." She gave me a dreamy smile.

I kissed her sleep softened lips. "My love, would you like us to stay here the night with your parents?"

She bit her lip and nodded.

I turned to Maeve. "We'd love to stay."

"Excellent. I have a pot of soup on the stove in the kitchen for dinner and I can whip up a pie for dessert if I can ever let go of this little guy." She kissed the baby on the forehead.

"Give him to me." Eamon held out his arms. "I haven't held my grandson yet."

Maeve smiled and placed Rian in his arms. Niamh stretched and sat up. Dia, she was even more beautiful now with her full breasts straining at the confines of her dress and a sleepy sensuality I usually only saw in our bed. My cock twitched. Niamh didn't miss the motion. She smiled with the same lust I had for her.

Rian wailed.

Eamon handed the baby to Niamh. "He sounds hungry. I'll get us lagers while we're waiting on dinner." He followed Maeve into the kitchen.

Niamh untied the front of her dress and offered her nipple to Rian. He latched onto it with a hunger I knew too well. I shifted on the couch and willed my cock to not jump to full mast, but it was hard with my mate's breast so ripe and creamy.

I cleared my throat. "How are you feeling?"

"Better after the nap."

"Good." I kissed her bare shoulder.

"We heal quick, Fintan, but hold that thought until we're not in my parents' house."

I chuckled. "I love you."

She raised her lips to mine. "I love you, too."

I kissed her as sweetly as I knew how, a promise, a taste of our love to come. For our love would continue to grow, and Niamh would always surprise me. She'd always be the mate meant for me.

PART THREE

A TRAGIC LOSS

CHAPTER NINETEEN

FINTAN

1700

D ID I BLINK? IT didn't feel like three hundred years since I'd found my mate. Three hundred years and five children. I couldn't believe our luck at having so many offspring. Two sons, princes, and future kings, and three daughters who were shining bright princesses that'd one day be future leaders too. If my father taught me one thing, it was the love of a mate that made an outstanding leader.

He'd taught me a lot of things.

But the one who'd taught me the most was Niamh.

She glided through the great hall in a storm-gray gown. The dress had tiny sleeves which wrapped around her slender arms. Attached to the back of the dress was a long, flowing expanse of gauzy material that fluttered behind her with every step, reminding me of a butterfly. The tight bodice hugged her breasts and nipped in at her waist. A waist I wanted to hold against mine all night while I teased her sensitive nipples with my fingers and tongue. The skirt shimmered with a layer of the same gauzy material over silk. Underneath, I'd find my mate bare as always.

After the ball tonight, I'd ravish her in her gown... and out of it.

"Mommy's a beautiful princess," Lorcan, our youngest son at two years of age, raced from behind her skirts.

"She is." I snagged Lorcan's arms and flung him up onto my shoulders. "She was a beautiful princess even before she became a real princess."

"I'm a prince." Lorcan wrapped his fingers in my crown. "Like you."

"Aye." I chuckled.

Niamh stopped in front of us, her face soft with love and indulgence.

"Hop down, baby," Niamh said. "Your mother and father are going to a ball tonight."

Saoirse, our youngest daughter at fourteen years of age, walked into the hall and lifted Lorcan from my shoulders.

"It's not fair." Saoirse pouted. "I want to go to a ball on Earth."

I lifted her chin. "You're much too young to go to a Water Sprite Ball, Saoirse. Your mother was too young at fifty. Do you think I'd let you go at fourteen?"

She placed Lorcan on her back piggyback style and bounced him up and down.

Lorcan squealed. "Giddy up, unicorn."

Saoirse scoffed. "You know the unicorns will never let us ride them."

Lorcan grabbed her hair and flicked it up and down.

Saoirse snorted like a horse and trotted off down the hallway. My heart swelled. They'd always be closer to each other than their other siblings.

I gathered Niamh into my arms and kissed her the way I'd wanted before I realized our youngest children were with her. She let out a throaty moan and sagged into my arms. I slid my hands under the cape attached to her dress, trailed them down her back, and cupped her buttocks.

"Would you two please not?" Aislinn, our middle daughter, said.

Niamh and I smiled against each other's lips and parted.

"At one hundred and forty-nine years of age, I would assume you'd know about sex by now." I raised an eyebrow. "If not, we should have a parental talk with you."

Aislinn's face flushed red. "Of course I know about sex," she spluttered.

Briana elbowed her sister. "You don't know about love though."

At one hundred and ninety-eight years old, our eldest daughter had been mated for many years. Her mate Donagh was a soldier in the King's guard, and they'd met when she was young. His dark reddish-brown hair matched his thirst for violence and fiery temper, and though I had my doubts about him, Briana was besotted with him—and he with her.

Aislinn poked her tongue out at Briana. Such childish behavior from Fae of their age, but our children always enjoyed the company of their siblings. Since Niamh and I were only children, we were rather lenient with their sibling dynamics. We didn't dictate how they acted with each other.

"Come, my precious daughters, walk with us to the great hall. Your grandparents insist you dine with them tonight."

"Grandmother always insists on feeding us," Briana said.

"It's easier to go with it."

Briana and Aislinn walked in front of us, elbowing each other the entire length of the hallway. Niamh rolled her eyes but smiled. My heart warmed with the love I held for her.

The King and Queen sat in the great hall, our eldest son, Rian, beside them. As he was next in line after me, Father had taken to training Rian in the way of kings and they shared a close bond. I didn't mind letting Father impart his wisdom to my son. The more knowledge, the better, and at two hundred and fifty years old, Rian had attained a lot of knowledge. All except the knowledge of his mate. I hadn't forced him to choose a mate when he turned two hundred, as my parents had with me. If I'd chosen another Fae woman the night of my birthday party, then I wouldn't have met Niamh, my fated mate. The draw she weaved over me kept me in awe of her, but I made sure to never show my weakness in front of the other Fae. I kept my worshipping of her for our bedroom. Or other places we found to be together alone.

"Mother, you look stunning." Rian stood.

"Thank you, Rian." Niamh kissed his cheeks.

Saoirse raced into the room with Lorcan still on her back. She plonked him in a seat, brushed her hair back from her face, slumping into the chair next to him.

"Saoirse, what is the matter?" King Diarmuid asked.

"I want to go to the ball." She met the King's gaze.

Oh, she was a force to be reckoned with as a teenager. I hoped one day she'd find a mate who could withstand her will.

The King's eyes narrowed into hard slits. "You want to go to a ball and become a mate in a Water Sprite harem?"

Saoirse's face paled.

"Your father didn't tell you what the ball was for?" the King asked.

Saoirse shook her head.

"Dia, Fintan. There's no point keeping knowledge from your children," he said. "It would have stopped this childish tantrum."

"She's fourteen," I said. "I didn't think she needed to hear about sex with multiple partners at her age. But I'll rectify that when we return."

"Father, no," Saoirse said.

Briana and Aislinn giggled. Saoirse glared at them. They'd likely end up with something rotten in their beds tonight. Saoirse didn't enjoy being left out, and she enjoyed being laughed at even less.

Mother stood and handed us our masks.

"Oh, yes, I left these in the sitting room," Niamh said. "Thank you."

Mother clasped Niamh's hands. "Be careful."

Niamh frowned. "We've been going to the ball for years, they are always a pleasant occasion."

"Except for the first one." I scowled.

Niamh tied my mask at the back of my head. "It wasn't entirely unpleasant for me."

I took her mask out of her hands and tied it around her face. "It was for me."

The night I rescued Niamh from the Water Sprite Ball would forever scar my mind, but when Axis, the Water Sprites Master, sent an invitation to his balls, we always accepted. For one, I wanted to flaunt our mating in his face and all his water sprites. Two, he was a fount of knowledge about Earth and the goings-on of humans. Three, we'd made a deal where he'd spy for our missing Fae in exchange for Niamh's singing. I'd passed what little knowledge he'd gathered onto the King and Queen, but Father still refused to acknowledge the threat building from the humans. I kept insisting he force all the Fae to return to the Summer Court. He wouldn't hear of taking away any Fae's choices.

And then there was my exquisite mate, who I'd kept this from for so long. How did I tell her now? And not have her think less of me? Possibly even lose her love? I couldn't risk losing her. She was my heart. Without her, I'd die.

"Are you ready, Niamh?" I parted the veil. "The ball won't wait for their most anticipated singer."

Niamh smiled in the way she did when she was about to sing for an audience. It filled her very being with happiness, and I'd do anything to make my mate happy.

We stepped through the shimmering silver haze of the veil and into the luminous blue of the Water Sprite's ballroom. The only reason I conceded to coming here was the powerful warding spells protecting this place he'd built after my unexpected arrival all those years ago. With the human threat worsening over the years, and without another realm to send his people to safety, the Water Sprite Master had become adept at defensive magic. He'd trained his people to blend with the water and become liquid ghosts when away from the Sprite Everglades. Besides making their home as safe as possible, they'd also become excellent spies and allies.

I led Niamh to the stage and watched her climb the stairs. She greeted the musicians, and soon her voice filled the ballroom. Water Sprites ventured onto the dance floor and swayed in a sensual rhythm to Niamh's words. The power in her voice had grown over the years, and she'd honed it to perfection to weave emotions and affect her audience with her singing. She could also blast our asses clear across the room with a surge of power, but tonight she sang about love and mating. Exactly why these Water Sprites were here, and she'd twine those emotions into her words.

I left Niamh on the stage and searched for Axis. He sat at a table with two women hanging onto his arms. Axis's dark brows dipped in a frown when he spotted me and tugged his arms out of the women's hands. With a nod to his left, I stepped through the packed tables and out of the ballroom.

Axis followed me into the reception area. "About time."

"Do you have any news this time?"

Axis glanced behind him. "Not here. Follow me."

He stalked into his office up to the fireplace and pushed a brick. The back of the fireplace creaked and swung open. Inside torches lined a dark tunnel.

"Where are we going?" I hissed.

"To the dungeons. There's someone I need to introduce you to."

"But Niamh?"

"She's safe in the ballroom. I have protected it with spells and posted guards at every entrance."

He ducked under the fireplace and into the tunnel. I followed him down the long, winding brick path. Every step past a glowing torch sent the flames waving and flickering long shadows on the walls. The further we walked, the closer the dull sound of moans echoed to us.

"Here we are." Axis opened a wrought-iron gate and waved me through.

I stepped through. Every hair on my body stood on end. Axis shut the creaking gate and continued past the many cells. Every cell held a being of some sort. I ignored them. This was Axis's realm, and they were his prisoners for reasons that didn't concern me.

"This one." He nodded at a cell with the door wide open. "This human here calls himself a Trapper."

I joined Axis at the cell door. Inside, they'd strapped a male human to a rack. Red blood ran in streams from under his armpits like his arms were about to be ripped off.

Axis stepped into the cell. "Speak, human."

The man lifted his head and snarled. "Fae."

"The Fae Prince, too," Axis goaded. "I bet you'd like to get your hands on him, wouldn't you?"

The man's lips snapped shut.

"Tell the Prince what you've been doing with his people."

The man said nothing.

Axis snapped his fingers and a stream of water flowed into the man's face. He spluttered and gasped for air until his lips turned blue. Axis clicked his fingers, and the water stopped.

"I... we... we're capturing Fae... to take their powers... we want to rule the Earth," the man stammered.

Power erupted from my hands. I clenched my fists and stepped inside the cell.

"How are you trying to take our powers?"

The man glared. "Burning. We believe flames will release your powers, but we hadn't figured out the right formula. But now. Now we have." He pulled on the restraints. "Soon we will be as powerful as you, and there's nothing you can do to stop us."

"Flames?" I bellowed. Fire crackled to my hands and up my arms. "Like this? Should I see what happens when I set you on fire?"

"Go ahead, Fae." He spat at my feet. "My people will rule the world and there's nothing you can do about it."

"We'll see about that." I stepped closer.

Luminous blue water encased my hands and snuffed out the flames.

"I can't let you kill my prisoner." Axis tipped his head and studied me. "Come, I'll tell you everything he's told us."

With an irritated huff, I stomped out of the cell. A minute longer in the man's presence and I wouldn't be able to stop my powers.

Axis led the way back out of the dungeons. "We stumbled across that idiot pissing in a stream, drunk and mumbling to himself about how powerful he'd be once he had the power of the Fae. My man captured him and brought him here."

"When?"

"Yesterday. I would have sent word, but I figured you were coming here tonight, anyway." He shrugged and led the way up the long corridor back to his office.

"How have they kept themselves hidden for so long?"

"Cloaking spells."

"Witches are helping them?"

"It would appear they involved witches." He ducked under the fireplace entrance.

"Did witches sell us out to the humans?" I followed behind him.

He shut the fireplace and perched on the edge of the desk. "Hard to say. We haven't finished interrogating him."

I folded my arms and leaned against the door.

Axis thrust a hand into his hair. "It's bad. We received more news that England, Germany, and Switzerland are missing entire Fae families. I assume the Trappers have burned them all."

I sucked in a shocked breath. "How did they keep this a secret for so long?"

"I suppose with them only taking one Fae here and there to experiment on, they led none of our searches to them, and the cloaking spells would have kept us all unaware." He thrust his hand through his hair again. "I don't like this one bit. I suggest you pull all your people back to the Summer Court. The way the man is talking, it sounds like they're gearing up for something big."

"I need to take proof to the King."

"I have no proof except piles of ashes he can see for himself if he'd ever leave the Summer Court," Axis spat. "I'm not putting my people at risk to get you any further proof. These humans are beyond insane, and one crazy crackpot in my dungeon is enough. You'll have to get it yourself."

"I can't very well take a human through the veil. The magic would kill him." I kicked the door, sending a loud thud throughout the room. "The King will just have to believe me if he doesn't want to come here and see the man for himself."

"You're screwed if he doesn't," Axis said. "I'll be happy to keep your mate safe here."

I clenched my fists and forced my power to stay put.

"She looks more beautiful every time I see her." He stood.

"Do you have to do this every ball?" I cocked an eyebrow.

"Of course." He brushed his knuckles down his bare stomach. "I'd love to have her in my harem."

I growled. Power flared into my hands, ready to rip him to pieces.

Axis chuckled. "So long as you protect her, I'll let her stay with you."

I snorted. "You think Niamh would leave me for you?"

"Hell, no. She'd blast my ass across the Earth if I got between you two, but it's always fun getting a rise out of you."

I wrenched my power back and shook my head. "One of these days, Axis."

"Come, let's enjoy your beautiful mate's singing before the shit show you're about to have when you return home."

"That's all you'll get to enjoy from her." I opened the door and strode out before I punched him.

I'd bring Niamh back to this office during the night and make sure Axis knew she was mine in every way. The Water Sprite Master was way too cocky for his own good. Maybe I should tell Niamh what he said just so she could send his ass flying—but having her in this room was way more appealing.

And then I'd have to convince my father of the human threat. The Trappers.

CHAPTER TWENTY

NIAMH

F INTAN'S RAISED VOICE EXPLODED through the drawing room door. In our three hundred and fifty years together, I'd never once heard him raise his voice. I grabbed the door handle.

"They're in danger," Fintan yelled.

A solid thud hit the door.

I jolted, my hand slipping from the handle. The door flung open. Fintan stopped in the doorway.

"Niamh?" He sighed.

"Who is in danger?" I asked.

Fintan glanced at the King standing behind him. The King's lips twitched into a tight line. Dread skittered down my spine.

"Who?" I demanded.

Fintan grasped my hand and drew me into the drawing room. The first time I'd ever been inside the men's private room. They respected our privacy too by never coming into our sitting room. Sometimes it was nice to have a place where I didn't have to deal with men. Thick, solid chairs sat in front of the ornate fireplace. A roar of blue fire crackled on the stones. No timber kept the flames alight—it was Fintan's powers making the fire. The King walked over to a desk under the window and shuffled papers into a drawer.

"Fintan?"

He flung his hand at the fire and the flames filled the fireplace.

I placed a hand on his arm. "What's wrong? Why are you letting your powers..." I waved my hand at the fireplace.

Fintan dropped his forehead against mine. "I... shite... I've kept something from you."

"What?" I tipped his face up with a hand. My stomach churned with guilt. He wasn't the only one keeping a secret. Perhaps now was the time to tell him mine?

"Earth isn't safe for Fae anymore."

"What do you mean?" I dropped my hand from his face, suddenly feeling like my limbs were lifeless. My parents lived on Earth. My entire family, outside of the Royals, lived on Earth.

"There are humans who... They call themselves Trappers. They seek to take our powers and rule Earth themselves." Fintan paced to the fireplace and gripped the mantle.

"Preposterous." I scoffed. "They can't take our powers." I swung to the King. "Can they?"

"No," King Diarmuid said. He didn't meet my eyes, though.

"How do they try to take our powers?" I swallowed the fear in my throat.

Silence from both men.

"How?" I demanded.

Fintan's hands glowed again. The fire sizzled to nothing with an icy blast. "They capture us and burn us at the stake."

I gasped and sunk into a chair. "We have to stop them."

"I've tried convincing Father of that for years."

"Years?" I stood up again and paced to Fintan. I placed my hand on his shoulder. "How many years?"

He rolled his shoulder under my hand. "Too many."

I dug my fingernails into his flesh. "Our children visit their grandparents. Are you telling me they've been in danger every time they leave the Summer Court?"

Fintan snorted. "Of course not. I send guards to keep watch. And the... occurrences have happened nowhere near their farm or even in Ireland."

I narrowed my eyes. "And this is the first I'm hearing of it?"

His lips pulled tight.

I clutched his shirt and pulled him closer. "Why?"

"Your parents made it clear they wouldn't leave their extended family and live here." His warm breath gusted over my face.

I blinked back the burn in my eyes.

"If they knew there was a risk to their lives—"

"Niamh," he said, his voice quiet. "Your father knew."

"No," I hissed. "I don't believe you."

"All I've ever wanted is to protect you, make sure you're happy."

My brows tugged into a frown. "You think keeping something of this magnitude did that?"

"I like to think you've been happy."

"I have been happy," I uttered.

"And if you'd known there was a possibility your parents were in danger? Would you have been happy?"

"I..." I snapped my mouth shut. Would I? Or would I have worried for years? Would that worry have marred my happiness with my mate?

"You forget," he said, tracing a finger over my temple. "I saw all your memories of your family. You love them so much."

He was right. And he was wrong to keep this from me.

I rounded on the King. "Why haven't we heard of this? Why haven't we done something?"

"There is nothing we can do," the King said. "We don't use our powers for destruction. We root them in the beauty of nature. I won't let us taint our powers."

"But you'll let us die." Fintan joined my side. "You'll let Niamh's family die."

"My family?" I screeched.

The power in my voice sent both men flying. They hit the wall with a shuddering thud. I raced over to Fintan and kneeled by his side.

"I didn't mean to hurt you."

"'Tis all right, Niamh, you have every right to be upset with me." He brushed my hair back from my face. "I should have told you sooner, regardless of what my father demanded. I should have insisted more that they live in the Summer Court."

I stood and paced the room. "That's why you kept asking them." I paused at the desk and wrenched open the drawer the King had put the papers in.

"No." The King lurched to his feet.

But it was too late. I'd read the first page. The paper listed names. Numbness filled my body, my fingers useless. The papers floated to the ground.

"Are these the names of the Fae who are dead because of the human Trappers?"

"Aye." The King swallowed hard. "We didn't know of their deaths until recently. I've sent word to every Fae settlement asking they reconsider living on Earth."

"You've sent word *asking?*" I stepped closer to him. "After all these deaths?"

"I keep telling him he should demand their return," Fintan said. "But he won't listen."

"I can't take away their choices, Fintan. That's not how one should act as a king. We lead, we don't force." He folded his arms over his chest.

"I thought we were meant to be the protectors of the Fae?" Fintan said.

"We are, son, we are." He unfolded his arms and clasped Fintan's shoulders. "We protect. We don't dictate. Dictators end up starting wars."

"Yet you had no qualms dictating I sing at Fintan's ball or the Water Sprites? Why can't you dictate now? Make your word a royal decree."

The King raised his eyebrows. "There is a difference."

"I fail to see it." I rubbed my hands down my dress. "My parents. I need to talk to my parents. Do they know they're in imminent danger on Earth?"

Fintan shrugged off his father's hands. "Niamh, you can't. It's too dangerous to leave the Summer Court."

"But?" I choked back a sob.

The King glanced away. Fintan's face softened.

"No." I waved my hand and reached for the veil.

Fintan clasped my hands in a firm grip and sealed the veil. "No. Niamh. You can't go to Earth. Think of the wee baby growing inside you."

Hot tears welled in my eyes. I ground my teeth.

"They'll come here. We have to believe that," Fintan said.

I ripped my hands out of his grip and yanked open the door. Our children scattered. Caught eavesdropping. I should be mad at them, but I was too upset. Too mad at my mate and the King. I ran down the hallway to our bedroom and threw myself across the bed. The tears fell, hot, angry blobs of wetness on my cheeks. I buried my face in the silk sheets.

"My love," Fintan whispered, and stroked my back. "Your parents will come here."

I wiped my face and sat up. "You've asked them to come here since we mated. Do you really think they'll come now?"

He brushed my damp cheeks with his thumbs. "I hope so."

My bottom lip trembled. "Hold me."

"Always." He gathered me into his arms on the bed.

I stared at the ceiling, seeing nothing but the faces of my parents, my aunts and uncles, nieces, and nephews. So many family members were in jeopardy. I needed to bring them here. I needed to go to Earth and warn them of the immediate danger. But Fintan wouldn't let me leave... unless. I started singing the soft lullaby my mother used to put me to sleep as a child, the song I'd sung to my children as babies. The song I sang to put my mate to sleep.

His breathing settled into a deep, even rhythm. I held onto him even though I was so mad at him. I understood his motivation, but my blood heated in my veins. Not once had he mentioned the brutalities on Earth. How bad could it be?

I slithered out of his arms and tiptoed across our bedroom. Fintan would understand when he woke. I'd go to my parent's farm for a few minutes. Tell them what was happening and bring them back here. I wouldn't even be away long enough for Fintan to know. He'd sleep through it all. A slight tremble in my hand made it slip off the handle on the first attempt at opening the door. I held my breath and clasped the handle, opened the door, and slipped through the small gap.

Our children, Rian, Briana, Aislinn, Saoirse, and Lorcan stood in the hallway, their faces etched with concern.

I stiffened my shoulders. "I'm going to Earth to get your grandparents."

"Mother, no," Rian said.

"Not here," I hissed, and hurried down the hallway.

The footsteps of my children followed me. I turned left into the next hallway and hurried faster, further away from my bedroom. If Fintan woke…

I sprinted to the heart of the palace. The atrium and our spring. The King and Queen faced each other, stormy expressions in the crackling atmosphere of power. Sparks of lightning flared above us. The Queen looked as angry as me.

Rian placed a hand on my arm.

"Niamh." The King stepped forward. "Fintan has tried for years to get your parents to live here."

"What could you possibly say to stop me from getting my parents?"

"Think of your mate and children."

"I am thinking of them," I seethed. "If you'd thought of them, you would have told me what was happening on Earth instead of keeping me oblivious. Instead of telling Fintan to not tell me."

"You don't understand." He placed his hand on mine.

I shook it off. "No, because you never told me. I thought I was a part of this family."

"Diarmuid," Queen Orlaith said. "Niamh has a point."

"What was I to do?" He turned to his mate. "Tell her all our royal secrets."

"She's our son's mate. She deserved to know." A bright flare of lightning and a crack of thunder accompanied her words.

"Enough of this." I waved my hand and called the veil. "This is wasting time."

"Mother, stop," Rian said. "You can't go if it's dangerous."

"Rian, my sweet boy, I'll be fine."

"I'll go with her," Briana said. "Maybe I can convince Grandmother."

Aislinn stepped forward. "I'll go too, I'm Grandfather's favorite."

Saoirse snorted. "Like we don't know that."

Lorcan ran from the atrium. Saoirse sprinted after him. Those two were off to get their father. He was the only one who'd stop me.

"Let's go." I stepped into the veil.

"I'm coming too," Queen Orlaith said.

"Shite," the King said before following us through the veil onto Earth.

CHAPTER TWENTY-ONE
FINTAN

"F ATHER, WAKE UP." LORCAN shook my shoulder. "Mother has gone."

"It's no good, Lorcan," Saoirse said. "She sang him to sleep, he'll be out for hours."

"Father," Lorcan yelled.

He shook me harder. I struggled against the hold sleep had on me. The urgent, panicked tone of his voice made me climb out of the darkness into the light where my children and mate were.

I sat up with a ragged jerk of limbs and forced open my eyes.

"Niamh?" I croaked.

"Mother went to Earth," Lorcan said.

My heart exploded in pain.

Rian stomped into the room. "Briana and Aislinn went too." He swallowed. "The King and Queen followed them."

After three hundred and fifty years and five children, you'd think I would have learned everything about my mate. But here it was, the one thing I'd feared since I'd found Niamh and she'd disappeared.

She was missing from the Summer Court again.

Our two oldest daughters, too. The ones who were closest to Niamh's parents and had spent the most time with them. It was little wonder they'd rushed to their grandparents.

And my parents. The King and Queen of all Fae.

"When did they go to Earth?" I bellowed.

"I told them not to go," Rian said. "We all did."

I spared a glance at Saoirse and Lorcan. The pair were a similar age to when I'd met Niamh. But Rian, he was older, he should have tried harder to stop them.

I focused on Niamh's mating mark etched on my chest. How had I not noticed she'd left the Summer Court? My limbs and head were sluggish with a sleepiness that wasn't normal. Did she sing me to sleep? Had she planned this trip to Earth? To her parents?

"Shite." My power flared and wavered.

Saoirse and Lorcan rushed to my side.

"I need to borrow a little power from you both." I clutched their hands. "It's hard fighting the power in Niamh's song."

"Take what you need, Father," Saoirse said.

"We'll go with you," Lorcan said. "We shouldn't have let Mother and the others go."

I nodded. Tugged on their powers, joined them with mine, stretched my power to the veil, and parted it.

"Rian, stay here. If anything happens to all of us, you're the future of the royals. The future of the Fae. The last protector."

"Father, no, I can help," Rian said.

"Do as I say. Please."

Rian kicked the wall, but nodded.

I stepped through the shimmering veil with Saoirse and Lorcan.

Earth was worse than I imagined.

Flames. So much fire crackled in the wood. The flare of bright orange flames licked up the pyres. Screams of pain. Of Fae burning alive. The scent of singed hair and flesh churned my stomach. I yanked on Saoirse's and Rian's power. With their hands clasped in mine, I sent an arctic blast over the flames. The fires sizzled and hissed to nothing, but the screams and crying grew louder in volume now there was no roar from the flames.

Niamh. Where was she?

My mating mark flared.

She was here.

Dia. No.

Not my Niamh.

Not her on one of these pyres.

I raced through the humans, frozen by my magic, standing around watching Fae die. My people. Humans did this. To my... no. My knees buckled, but I stayed on my feet. My parents' blackened dead faces stared at each other from separate pyres. Beside them, on more pyres, Niamh's dead parents. I forced steel into my legs. Beside me, Saoirse and Rian sobbed. I blocked out the noise. I couldn't comfort them now. Not when...

There.

My mating mark flared with warmth.

My throat stopped working, my lungs ceased breathing in the ash-tinted air.

She couldn't be dead. Her skin was red and blistered, her hair singed to nothing. They'd burned her severely.

Niamh. I silently cried her name for no words would come.

Her red eyelids opened and closed.

She was alive.

But...

I clambered over the burned wood, snapped the pole the Trappers had strapped her to, and swung her up into my arms.

"Children," Niamh whispered.

Feck.

I glanced at the pyre on the other side of her. Saoirse worked on freeing Briana, and the next pyre over Lorcan worked on freeing Aislinn. Both appeared unharmed, but the scars of this night would run deeper than this moment.

"I need to get you to the spring," I said. "The children will be close behind us."

Niamh sagged in my arms. I didn't dare wait another moment. I parted the veil, entered the atrium, ran to the spring, and sank into the running water. With great care, I used my power to run the water over every inch of her skin. Gradually, her skin healed. I peeled her blackened clothes off her body so the healing water could get to her skin better.

Saoirse appeared with Briana, easing her burned feet into the spring's healing water.

"Where's Lorcan and Aislinn?"

"They were right behind me." Saoirse frowned. "I'll go back." She stepped through the veil.

Much later, Lorcan and Saoirse returned with Aislinn. Her pale skin was whiter than the moonlight. Aislinn looked like she suffered from shock.

"What happened?" I demanded.

Aislinn cleared her throat. "We thought we'd go to Earth and get Grandfather and Grandmother. Bring them back here to be safe. The Trappers were waiting for us. They used some sort of spell to capture us and then they..." she gulped. "They set us on fire one at a time." Tears streamed down her cheeks.

Saoirse wrapped her arms around Aislinn's shoulders and let her sob.

"Children," Niamh gasped.

"They're here," I said. "Hush, my love. Heal first."

Her pink eyelids snapped open. "Our parents..."

"I saw." I clenched my jaw. "Briana, get a sleeping potion. This is too painful for your mother."

Briana walked away from the spring, her feet healed to perfection. She returned in moments and handed me a vial. I eased Niamh's raw lips apart and tipped the contents into her mouth. She gulped, choked, coughed, swallowed. Then she was asleep.

Rian rushed into the atrium. His face blanched when he saw his mother, but I couldn't tell him she'd be all right when I didn't know it for myself.

"Grieg," I yelled. my voice so loud and powerful, it reverberated through every inch of the palace.

Grieg appeared in the atrium, took the scene in with one glance and ran to my side. "Prince Fintan, what happened?"

"Humans," I hissed. "They killed the King and Queen. Gather the King's Guard, we're going to war."

"Aye, King Fintan." He bowed. "Donagh left for Earth a short while ago when he heard Briana was there."

"My mate is on Earth?" Briana's hands glowed.

Grieg took a step back. "I'll gather the guards."

"Briana," I snapped. "Come, hold your mother in the spring until her skin fully heals."

Briana scowled but swapped places with me. I needed her here with her mother, not on Earth where the unthinkable might happen again.

"Father, find Donagh for me, please," Briana begged.

"I will, and I'll end every human that is against us." I strode from the spring in my damp clothes, uncaring how the fabric clung to my body. "Something I should have done years ago."

"I'm going with you," Lorcan said, standing tall.

I nodded. We hurried through the palace to the courtyard, where every royal guard stood waiting for their command.

"Humans calling themselves Trappers have targeted us. They killed your King and Queen. The Trappers killed your friends and family. My friends and family. We will end this tonight."

The guards lifted their glowing swords and hollered their battle cries.

I parted the veil with the brightest silver power of my life. One by one, we stepped through the blinding light. Before we annihilated the Trappers, I needed to find out if the witches truly had sold us out to the humans. If they had, then they were another enemy we needed to destroy.

"Where are we?" Lorcan asked.

The weeping willow trees swayed in a vicious breeze. The scent of distant smoke tainted the air. We weren't near any pyres, but there must have been so many fires tonight they'd filled the Earth with the horrific aroma.

"Earth. England, to be precise." I strode through the forest. "This way."

Lorcan hurried to keep up with my long strides. We exited the forest. Saltine's house sat in a heap with a collapsed side wall, the roof leaned at an angle, the front door wide open on one hinge.

"Shite, whose house is this?"

"Saltine, our witch aide."

Lorcan whistled through his teeth. "Do you think she's still alive?"

I shrugged and walked to the door. A low moan escaped from a pile of rubble. Lorcan and I rushed to the collapsed corner of the roof and dug through the bricks. Familiar black hair came into view. I wrenched the rubble away with a surge of my powers.

"Saltine."

She struggled to sit up.

I scooped an arm under her back and lifted her. "You're injured. You should lay still."

"There's no time." She patted a shaky hand down her front to the pouch at her waist. Her fingers snapped it open and pulled out a vial. "Outside." She coughed. Blood trickled from her mouth. "There's a Trapper with my dagger in his side." She brushed the blood from her chin and wiped it on her dusty clothes. "He should be dead. I need a drop of his blood to finish this potion. Go, boy."

Lorcan looked at me. I nodded my head at the door. He scrambled to his feet and ran outside.

"What happened?" I asked.

"A Trapper came to capture me." She cackled. "They should have sent more than one." She spat blood on the floor. "You came for answers, and a potion."

"Aye." I eased her against the wall and sat back on my haunches. "I heard the Trappers used magic to capture us, and they've been using cloaking spells to hide. Are witches working with them?"

"Not by choice. Some idiots they captured made potions in exchange for their lives." She scowled. "From what I've heard, the Trappers killed them anyway."

"So the witches condemned us to death for nothing?" My power swirled to my hands.

Saltine placed her hand over mine. "Not for nothing, King Fintan."

I raised my eyebrows. How had she learned of my father's death already?

Lorcan rushed back through the door with a bloody dagger. "Is this it?"

"Yes, little warrior." Saltine uncorked the vial. "Dip it in here."

Lorcan kneeled on the other side of Saltine and dipped the blade into the clear potion. The liquid bubbled and turned dark blue.

"Drink it." She pushed the vial at Lorcan.

"Wait." I placed my hand on top of the vial. "What is it for?"

"It's a potion to track anyone with Trapper's blood. No cloaking spell will hide them from this. You'll be able to do what you came to Earth for."

"What?" Lorcan asked.

"To kill them, of course," Saltine said.

"I should drink it." I tightened my hand on the vial.

"No, Fintan. You're King of the Fae—this isn't your destiny," Saltine said.

"Give it to me." Lorcan tugged the vial. "Father, you need to lead our people now. Rian is next in line. I'm expendable if this doesn't work."

Saltine huffed. "My potions always work. Just ask your mother."

Lorcan frowned. I let go of the vial. He didn't wait—he tipped the vial to his lips and drank the potion. I waited for him to scream in pain as Niamh had done so long ago, but Lorcan smiled.

"It tasted like blueberries," he said.

Saltine withdrew a black vial from her pouch. "A drop of this potion will stop witch's magic affecting you."

"This is what I came here for." I snatched one and placed a drop on the tip of my finger before placing it in my mouth.

Lorcan did the same.

Saltine cackled. "I know. Why do you think I already made it?"

"Is there anything we can do for you?"

"No, leave me to my fate." She waved her hand.

I stood in a rush. Now she'd protected us from witch magic and made Lorcan a tracker for the Trappers, we could put an end to this.

"I'll bring you back payment for your services."

Saltine placed a hand on Lorcan's arm. "Wait. I have something for you."

"What?" Lorcan asked.

Saltine pointed at the grimoire on the floor beside the overturned cauldron. "Take my grimoire. I can't protect it in my state and one day my descendants will need it. You will give it to them."

"When?" he asked.

"Everyone wants to know when." She sighed and slumped lower against the wall. "I'm tired." She coughed, sending a trail of fresh blood trickling from the corner of her mouth.

"Saltine?" Lorcan shook her shoulder.

I turned away and strode outside. Time to give the King's guards, my guards, a drop of the potion too. Then we'd all be ready. There was so much death here on

Earth, and we were about to create more. The direction of my thoughts would horrify Father, but his blacked dead face flashed in my mind. My mother's, too. I stiffened my spine. The Trappers had brought this on themselves.

Lorcan stomped from the crumpled house, the leather-bound grimoire in his hands. The book lit up a sparkling midnight blue and shrunk in size to that of a notebook. He stared at it in awe.

"Lorcan." I placed a hand on his shoulder.

He tucked the book into his pocket. "I'm ready, Father." Lorcan pointed in the opposite direction of the forest. "There are Trappers that way."

I faced the guards. "The witch has given us an advantage. We are immune to their spells and Lorcan can now lead us straight to our enemy, the Trappers." I called a sword of flames to my hand. "I want them to suffer."

Lorcan produced twin swords of flames and led the way. I might be King, but he was my son. I wouldn't let him do this alone, and with the entire King's guard at our backs, we'd incinerate every Trapper alive on Earth. Just as they'd sought to destroy us, we'd bring vengeance and fury. Swords and death. Flames too.

CHAPTER TWENTY-TWO
FINTAN

I STRODE INTO OUR bedroom, stripped my blood and ash-covered clothes from my body. When I saw Niamh still sound asleep in our bed, I paused.

I'd almost lost her.

I stumbled into our bathroom and washed the remainders of death and destruction from my body. Naked, I slid into the bed beside my mate.

"Fintan." Niamh clutched at my body with tight fists.

"Shhh, I'm here."

She blinked open her pale eyelids, still missing her lashes. Her hair was missing too, but the painful red blisters had healed and her skin was back to flawless pale.

"I fixed everything. You don't need to worry. No one will ever hurt you or our family again."

"I'm sorry," she whispered.

"Me too." Tears welled in my eyes. "Our parents are dead. Briana's mate Donagh is dead." I swallowed. "Our grandbaby Deidre is dead."

"No. Not Deidre too." She sobbed, her shoulders shaking with the force of her grief. "It's all my fault. I should have stayed. I should have listened to you."

"It's my fault too. I should have stopped the Trappers sooner. Insisted Father command all Fae to the Summer Court and seal the veil." I laid back on the bed and placed an arm over my eyes. "I should have ignored his commands and told you sooner."

"Yes, you should have."

"Will you ever forgive me?" I whispered.

"Oh, Fintan. I'm angry at you for not telling me, but." She sighed. "I already have forgiven you."

I swallowed the lump in my throat. "I'm King now and you're Queen of the Fae."

Niamh laid her head on my chest over her mating mark. Warmth seeped into my body that hadn't been there since the moment I'd woken and found her missing.

I placed a hand on her stomach. "The baby?"

She placed her hand on top of mine. "The baby is unharmed."

I puffed out a tiny breath of relief. We'd only conceived this baby a few days ago.

"I'll do whatever you say from here on out," she whispered.

Her voice still sounded injured from the fire. My heart ached with pain for her, for what I'd almost lost.

I slid my other arm over her back and held her tight.

"I almost lost you." A sob burst free.

"I'm sorry, Fintan. So sorry." She kissed her mating mark on my chest. "I love you. Don't hate me because I tried to save my parents."

"I don't hate you. I'd never hate you." My arms moved to hug her tighter. "I love you, Niamh. Forever."

Her warm, wet tears landed on my chest.

"It's humans I hate, but that doesn't matter now, I sealed the veil. No Fae can ever leave the Summer Court, and no one from Earth can ever come in. We're safe."

We held each other and shed the tears for those we lost. After the Trappers and their night of mass pyres, more than half the Fae population was gone, their lives up in flames in a matter of minutes.

Now we were safe in the Summer Court... but as grief and exhaustion dragged us toward sleep, I couldn't help but wonder what the future held for Fae.

And our royal children.

CHAPTER TWENTY-THREE
EPILOGUE
FINTAN 1975

"Ready or not, here I come," she called.

A tiny giggle sounded to her right.

I peered around the tree I was hiding behind and winked at our youngest daughter, Roisin, five years old and the lightest of souls born in the Summer Court since I'd sealed us in. The last two-hundred and twenty-five years had been peaceful. Quiet. We'd mourned those first years, but we'd embraced the life we had.

Niamh spun in the opposite direction to Roisin and pounced around a tree.

"Found you," she said.

"Mother," Saoirse groaned. "Why do you always find me first?"

"Because you never hide well enough."

"I do too." She pouted and pointed at a tree.

She'd never lost her stubborn, rebellious streak. Especially when it came to outdoing her brothers and sisters, and even more when trying to best me in a sword fight. She was brilliant with her power over water, and the swords she made from water would even delight Axis.

Since that devastating night, our children had chosen to only use one power like the rest of the Fae population. I understood their insistence they focus on one of their powers and not use the others. We'd failed our people that night. So many had died before we'd put an end to the Trappers.

We were royals though, we should use all our powers. But I made sure they'd honed the power they chose to perfection. In defense and attack. I wouldn't take any chances with their lives. If I wasn't there to protect them, then they could protect themselves.

Niamh tiptoed to the next tree.

"Found you." She grabbed hold of Lorcan's arm.

"You ratted me out, didn't you?" Lorcan scowled.

Saoirse shrugged.

"Why you." He ran at Saoirse.

She ducked to the side, and they tried to land smacks on each other's heads. It was good to see Lorcan play after what I'd made him to do to the human Trappers. The night we'd returned covered in our enemy's remains, I wasn't sure if it tarnished him for life. With the way he'd focused his power on fire, it was still a possibility.

He clipped Saoirse's ear and grinned. She threw up her hands in defeat. I chuckled. Niamh spun in my direction. I stood ramrod straight and didn't breathe.

Niamh's footsteps padded across the ground in the opposite direction. I nodded my head at Roisin and we scampered to different trees. I lost sight of her, but she was safe in the Summer Court.

"Found you," Niamh's voice rang out through the forest.

"Mother," Briana said. "Can I go back to the castle now?"

"No," Niamh said. "You're a part of this family."

Daisies burst from the ground, a sure sign Briana's power got the better of her. Briana had suffered an even worse loss, her mate and child. Her sad days were bleak, and she'd used her power over plant life like it was the one thing keeping her going.

Aislinn sneezed. "Damn you, Briana." She stepped out from behind a tree. "That's cheating."

Aislinn never spoke of that night. No matter how hard her mother and I tried to get her to open up, she was adamant she never wanted to talk about it. I feared she'd never accept what had happened if she never talked about it, but her inner strength was the strongest I'd ever seen. She reminded me a lot of my mother.

"It's only cheating if I'm the one searching," Briana said.

A flash of light to my right took my attention off their bickering. Rian used his powers to draw soil up from the ground and covered himself, adding an extra layer to his hiding.

"Found you, Ciara," Niamh said.

"Shite, the sun gave me away today," Ciara said.

She'd honed her skill with shadows, and she could disappear into the darkness. I feared she'd chosen that power as a marker. They'd injured her when the Trappers burned Niamh alive while pregnant with her. But the one boy who'd been born the same year as her kept her from totally disappearing into the darkness. Yet, I wasn't sure if their relationship was romantic.

"Found you." Niamh swung around the tree Rian hid behind and brushed the dirt from his face.

He waved his hand, and the soil returned to the ground. My father's death had hurt Rian the most, and as the eldest prince, he was one step closer to being King himself. He'd grown more and more secretive over the years, hiding away from everyone for longer than what should be possible in the Summer Court. But he'd proven how good he was at hiding when playing hide and seek.

"That you did, Mother." Rian kissed her cheek.

"Two left," Niamh said.

A giggle echoed from my left.

"I wonder who will win hide and seek?" Niamh's voice grew closer.

Roisin giggled again, but Niamh kept heading my way. Her sweet scent grew stronger. I breathed her in like she was the reason for living. And she was. She stepped around the tree; her face alight with a cheerful smile.

"Found you," she said, her voice taking on a huskier note than when she said it to our children.

I took advantage of our seclusion, placing my hands on her waist and dragging her against my body.

"You did." I lowered my voice. "Now what are you going to do?"

Niamh stretched up and placed her lips on mine. I deepened the kiss, swiping my tongue along the seam of her lips and into her mouth. She opened to me as she always did. A claiming of mates.

"Mommy, come find me," Roisin called.

Our lips stretched into a smile against each other's. Niamh stepped back, turned on her heel, and raced around the tree.

"I'm coming to get you last, Princess."

Roisin squealed in delight. "I won."

Niamh caught her up in her arms and spun her around in the sunlight streaming through the trees. She was the picture of joy, my happiness, and I'd do anything to keep her happy. Whatever we'd endured, we'd always have this. Us. Our family. And our love.

As I took in the faces of our children and the lack of the contentment I possessed with a mate by my side, a flare of unease twitched the royal powers. My palms glowed silver, reaching for the locked veil. I slapped them together, drawing my power back.

I should make them all choose a mate. If only to be as happy as me and Niamh.

I shook my head. Not yet. But the time would soon come, the princes and princesses would need to decide on a mate for the future of our people. For the royal family. And themselves.

Read on to discover how Fintan and Niamh's children find their fated mates and help to save the Fae from a greater threat.

FATED MATES OF THE FAE ROYALS

1. Fae's Song

2. Fae's Wolf

3. Fae's Alpha

4. Fae's Heart

5. Fae's Witch

6. Fae's Dream

7. Fae's Fate

8. Fae's Love

Acknowledgments

First, thank you to my family for putting up with me disappearing into the world of books. To Belinda, thank you for encouraging me to write again after I lost everything in a computer crash. Remember to back up! A lot of work goes into creating a story, and I'm always thankful for the support of my online writing buddies, beta readers, and fellow authors, Immy for always making me smile, Tammy for believing in me from the start, Karen for being willing to read any level of heat I write. Cassie for her hand holding. Lana for her invaluable knowledge. Also, my fabulous beta reader Erica and her help with US English. The biggest thank you goes to my 'twin' Dannielle, who is the best critique partner, cheerleader, and sounding board ever, and is forever fixing my comma errors, sorry Dannielle I'm afraid you're stuck with them and me. Finally thank you to all you romance readers. You are my tribe.

ALSO BY

Anthologies

Reluctant Bride

Alpha Male

ABOUT AUTHOR

Helen Walton is a tea drinking, chocoholic, romance writer. Stories are her obsession. She adores creating sensual romances containing a sprinkling of humor and the all-important happy ending. She lives in South Australia with her family, and menagerie of quirky animals where they all take her away from her book world and demand to be fed. Lucky for them, she enjoys cooking but prefers baking.

Sign up for my newsletter for exclusive content.

https://www.helenwaltonauthor.com/newsletter

Visit my website

https://www.helenwaltonauthor.com/

Follow me

BB bookbub.com/profile/helen-walton

f facebook.com/Helen-Walton-Author-1034966677
06602/

g goodreads.com/author/show/20249188.Helen_Wa
lton

⊙ instagram.com/helen.walton.author

♪ tiktok.com/@helen.walton.author